SHADOW HUNT

SHADOW POINT SECURITY ROMANTIC
SUSPENSE SERIES
BOOK 1

MISTY EVANS

CHAPTER ONE

Garrett
The Last Stand Bar & Grille
Blackridge, Montana

NAVY SEAL COMMANDER GARRETT CROSS was three whiskeys in when the person who was about to change his life forever sat on the barstool next to him.

He didn't look up from the amber liquid he'd been nursing for the past twenty minutes. The Last Stand wasn't the kind of place where strangers made conversation. It was where you came to be left alone with your demons and a bottle.

Garrett had plenty of demons.

The jukebox in the corner played something country and melancholic. A handful of locals occupied tables near the back, their voices a low murmur beneath the music. Jake, the bartender, knew better than to ask if

Garrett wanted another. He'd pour when the glass was empty. Until then, he stayed on the other end of the bar, polishing glasses that didn't need polishing.

The September evening had cooled after a warm day, the kind of temperature that reminded you fall was coming to Montana, whether you were ready or not. Through the window on his left, Garrett could see the sun setting behind the mountains, painting the sky in shades of orange and purple.

He didn't give a shit about the sunset.

Eighteen months since the Navy had kicked him out. Eighteen months of wondering if the kill had been worth his career, his reputation, his entire life.

It had been. He'd do it again.

That's why he was here, drinking cheap whiskey in a nowhere town, instead of leading his team on some op halfway around the world.

The door opened, letting in a gust of cool air that carried the scent of pine and approaching cold nights. Garrett's old instincts fired before his brain caught up. In the mirror behind the bar, he catalogued the newcomer while appearing as if he didn't care.

Female. Five-three, maybe five-four in the heels clicking across the worn wooden floor. Expensive perfume—something subtle that didn't belong in a dive bar. Designer coat. East Coast money, judging by the way she carried herself.

And she was walking straight toward him.

Shit.

The woman slid onto the stool next to him without

asking permission. Up close, she was mid-thirties with dark hair pulled back, intelligent brown eyes that assessed him the way he'd just evaluated her, and a wedding ring on her left hand.

Jake appeared, eyebrows raised. "What can I get you?"

"Water, please." Her voice confirmed the East Coast thing. Cultured. Confident. "With lemon, if you have it."

Jake nodded and disappeared to get her order. The woman settled into her seat, crossed her legs, and waited.

Garrett didn't acknowledge her presence. If she wanted something, she could start the conversation. He felt the itch to move to a booth. To get away from her. But he wasn't going to give her the satisfaction of causing him to so much as twitch. He went back to his whiskey.

Thirty seconds of silence. A full minute. Two.

Finally, "Garrett Cross?"

He didn't answer. Took another drink instead.

"I'm Dr. Genevieve Montgomery."

"Not interested."

"You don't even know what I'm offering."

"I know I don't want it." He still hadn't looked at her.

She made a soft sound that might have been amusement. From the corner of his eye, he watched her pull a folder from the leather bag she'd set on the floor. She placed it on the bar between them, her movements unhurried.

He didn't look at it. She opened it anyway. The photograph on top made ice slide down his spine.

It showed the Colombian jungle. Tactical gear. Him.

The dead body of a serial killer.

Everything in him went utterly still. That photo shouldn't exist. The mission had been off the books, the evidence scrubbed, the witnesses paid off. He'd covered his tracks so thoroughly that his own command couldn't prove what he'd done.

But here it was. Proof.

His hand tightened on the glass. Every muscle in his body tensed, his internal threat assessment cranking into overdrive.

Who the hell is she? Who does she work for?

"Colombia," she said, her tone conversational. "Eighteen months ago. You went off-mission for twelve hours."

Garrett said nothing.

"Local women were disappearing from villages near your operational area. Turning up dead. Tortured." She paused. "You tracked the killer to his compound in the jungle."

His gut cramped. "You telling me or asking me?"

"I'm telling you I know what you did. And I know you left no evidence."

Except that damned photo she had. He finally looked at her. Really looked. Those intelligent eyes were steady on his face, reading him the way a psychologist reads patients. No fear or judgment. Just calm assessment.

"Then you don't know anything," he said.

A small smile touched her lips. "I know you killed a predator the Colombian authorities couldn't touch because of political connections. I know you saved lives that night. And I know your command suspected what you'd done but couldn't prove it, so they branded you a rogue operative and cut you loose." She leaned forward slightly. "I also know you'd do it again in a heartbeat."

Garrett picked up his glass, finished the whiskey in one swallow. The burn down his throat was familiar. Comforting. "What do you want, Doc? I'm not interested in therapy."

"Good, because I'm not offering it." She slid another photograph toward him. "I'm offering you this."

It was a professional headshot of a woman with the US flag behind her. FBI credentials visible. A woman with brunette hair pulled back, serious blue eyes, and the kind of beauty that came with competence and intelligence.

The eyes and the name on the badge stopped his heart.

Special Agent Claire Dawson.

Time stopped.

The bar faded. The music disappeared. Everything narrowed to that photograph and the name beneath it.

Claire Josephine Dawson. Lily's best friend, CJ.

He couldn't breathe for a second. His hand, still on the bar, had gone numb. Every nerve in his body fired at once—recognition, shock, and something that felt uncomfortably like panic.

He hadn't seen her in fifteen years. Not since Lily's funeral. Not since she'd looked at him with those guilt-stricken blue eyes and whispered 'I'm sorry' over and over until he'd had to walk away before he broke down in front of everyone.

She'd been fourteen. Skinny, with a broken arm in a cast, a concussion, and tears that wouldn't stop. Just a kid who'd tried to save his sister and failed.

Now she was an FBI agent.

Jesus Christ.

"You know her." Not a question. A statement.

Garrett forced himself to swallow. Forced his voice to work. "What about her?"

"She's in trouble. The kind of trouble the FBI can't handle through official channels."

He dragged his gaze from the photo to the woman beside him. "The Feds have more than enough resources."

"Not the kind I have." She paused. "Correction. Not like you and I *both* have."

What the hell did she want from him? "I'm retired."

"You're thirty-three years old and drinking yourself to death in Montana." Her voice was gentle but firm. "That's not retirement. That's surrender."

The words hit harder than they should have. Garrett looked away, back to Claire's photo. FBI agent—she'd made something of herself. Built a career hunting predators.

Just like he had. "Why are you showing me this?"

Dr. Montgomery pulled out more photographs. Crime scene photos. Three women, all brunette, all with similar features.

All dead.

"Claire is being stalked," she said quietly. "The pattern matches these three victims. All were contacted by the stalker weeks before they were killed. All were taunted. All died within days after the final message."

Garrett's tactical mind engaged despite his resistance. He studied the photos, seeing what the psychologist wanted him to see. The similarities. The escalation. The methodical patience of a predator who planned every move.

These women looked like Claire. One of them could have been her.

His knuckles had gone white on the edge of the bar.

"FBI has behavioral analysts," he said, his voice rougher than it should be. "Protective details."

"They're protecting her. Officially. By the book." Dr. Montgomery tapped one of the crime scene photos. "This predator isn't playing by that book. He's organized, patient, and he's been watching Claire for months. Maybe years."

"What makes you think I can stop him?"

"Because you've done it before. Without permission. Without rules." She tapped the Colombia photo. "You hunt monsters, Garrett. That's what you're good at."

"I'm done hunting."

"Are you?" She held his gaze. "Or are you just hiding?"

Jake set her water in front of her and disappeared again, sensing the tension radiating from Garrett. Smart man.

Claire's serious blue eyes stared at him from the photo. She was professional. Composed. Nothing like the terrified fourteen-year-old he remembered.

But somewhere behind that FBI agent's mask, she was still CJ. Still Lily's best friend and the girl who'd fought a killer with a broken arm and survived.

"Tell me about Shadow Force International," he said.

If Dr. Montgomery was surprised he knew the name, she didn't show it. She did seem to choose her words carefully. "We handle private security and intelligence operations for clients who need discretion."

"Private military."

"That's the public face." She straightened slightly. "My branch, Shadow Point Security, is different. It's a new unit within SFI. We specialize in domestic threats—predators that law enforcement can't shut down fast enough. Serial killers. Stalkers. Traffickers. The monsters hiding in plain sight."

"Vigilante justice."

"Preemptive, you might say. Justice that gets results." She met his eyes. "You believe in that. You proved it in Colombia."

"And it cost me my career."

"I'm offering you a new one. One where doing the right thing doesn't get you court-martialed." She pulled a white business card from her pocket and set it on top of Claire's photo. "I need a tactical commander for Shadow Point. Someone who understands how predators think. Someone who won't hesitate to cross lines when necessary."

"Someone expendable if it all goes sideways."

"Someone *capable*." She stood, smoothing her coat. "Claire doesn't have much time. Days, maybe. The stalker sent his first direct message three days ago. His previous victims were dead within a week of first contact."

Garrett's stomach went cold. Three days.

"The FBI knows she's next," she continued. "They've assigned a protective detail. They're doing everything by the book. But this predator has already circumvented their security twice. Left messages for Claire where no one should have been able to reach her."

She picked up her bag, left cash on the bar for the water she hadn't touched.

"When you change your mind—and you will—call that number." She nodded to the business card. "I have an official office front in town, a compound outside the city limits. I'll be at the office tomorrow morning. Eight a.m."

"I'm not coming."

"Yes, you are." She smiled, but there was something sad in it. "Because you can't live with another failure. And if Claire Dawson ends up dead while you're hiding in this bar, you'll never forgive yourself."

She stopped for a moment and patted his shoulder. "I did my research on you, Garrett. I know about Lily. I know Claire was her best friend. And I know that's why you'll show up tomorrow."

She strode to the door. Another gust of cool September air rushed in, then disappeared.

Garrett sat frozen, staring at the photographs. The three dead women. The Colombia mission. Claire's FBI badge.

I know about Lily.

His hands shook.

He grabbed the folder, shoved everything back inside. The white business card fell out, landing face-up next to his empty glass. No name or company logo. Just a phone number and address.

He should burn it. Should walk out of this bar, drive to his cabin, and forget Dr. Genevieve Montgomery and her Shadow Point Security team existed.

But Claire's photo was staring up at him from inside the folder.

Those blue eyes that had been full of guilt at Lily's funeral. That had silently asked Bobby for forgiveness. Bobby—the name she'd known him by—hadn't been able to give it. That had haunted him every day for fifteen years.

"Hell," Garrett muttered.

Jake materialized. "Another?"

Garrett looked at his empty glass. Looked at the folder. Looked at the door.

I can't. I failed Lily. I can't face CJ.

Bobby couldn't save his sister. Garrett couldn't save Claire.

But the memory came anyway. Always did, especially when the whiskey wasn't working.

Lily at ten years old, making him promise. "If anything ever happens to me, Bobby, you'll take care of CJ, right?"

"Nothing's going to happen to you, Lil."

"But if it does. Promise."

"I promise."

Eight years later, he'd broken that promise. Stood at his sister's grave while CJ cried, apologized, and blamed herself for surviving.

He'd enlisted the next day. Became Garrett Cross— his father's surname, his first name. No more Bobby. He became someone strong enough, lethal enough, skilled enough that he'd never fail to protect someone who needed it again.

And now CJ needed protection.

"No thanks," he told Jake. He threw money on the bar, grabbed his jacket and the folder, and headed for the door.

Outside, the evening had cooled further. The parking lot gravel crunched under his boots as he walked to his beat-up Ford. Above, stars were beginning to appear in the darkening sky. Montana stars, brilliant and endless without light pollution to dim them.

He got in the truck. Didn't start it. Just sat there with the folder on the passenger seat and his hands on the steering wheel.

Through the bar window, he could see Jake collecting glasses. A couple at one of the back tables laughing at something. Normal people living normal lives.

Garrett hadn't been normal since Lily died.

Dr. Montgomery's words echoed in his head. *You're thirty-three years old and drinking yourself to death in Montana. That's not retirement. That's surrender.*

She was right. He'd been surrendering for eighteen months. Hiding. Running from the ghosts that followed him from Colombia, from the Teams, from the life he'd built after Lily.

But he couldn't run from this.

He opened the folder again. Claire's photo was on top. Professional. Competent. Alive.

For now.

She had days, maybe.

His jaw clenched. His hands tightened on the steering wheel until his knuckles cracked.

Three women were dead. Claire was next. And somewhere out there under the same stars was a stalker who'd been watching her for months. FBI protection that wasn't good enough.

And Lily's plea echoing across fifteen years. *Take care of CJ.*

He'd failed once. Lily was dead because he hadn't been there, hadn't protected her, hadn't been strong enough or fast enough or good enough.

But Claire was still alive.

And Dr. Montgomery was right—he couldn't live with himself if he let her die too.

"Goddammit," Garrett said to the empty truck.

He pulled out his phone. Looked at the business card Dr. Montgomery had left. Looked at Claire's photo.

Lily's voice in his head: *Promise.*

"I promise, Lil," he whispered.

Pocketing his phone, he started the truck. He didn't drive toward his cabin in the woods. Instead, he headed toward the address on the card.

The office on Main Street was small, discreet. Most

people probably thought it was just another boring security company.

The lights were still on in the second-floor windows. Garrett parked across the street and stared up at them. Dr. Montgomery was up there, waiting. Knowing he'd come.

I did my research on you, Garrett.

She'd played him perfectly. Showed him the Colombia photo to prove she had leverage. Showed him Claire to prove she had bait. Told him about Lily to prove she knew exactly which buttons to push.

And it had worked.

Because at the end of the day, he wasn't Bobby anymore—the kid who'd failed his sister. He was Garrett Cross. Former SEAL. Predator hunter. The man who'd crossed every line in Colombia to stop a monster.

And he'd cross them again to keep Claire Dawson alive.

Even if she never knew Bobby was the one protecting her.

He grabbed the folder, got out of the truck, and crossed the street. The door to the building was unlocked. Stairs led up to the second floor. At the top, a frosted glass door was devoid of any title or name.

Covert as hell. Fine, then.

He didn't knock. Just opened the door and walked in.

A reception desk sat empty. Down a short hall, he saw the lights on. He moved quietly and found Dr. Montgomery behind a desk, reading something on her computer. She looked up when he entered, and her expression didn't change. "Commander Cross," she said. "Sooner than I expected. Come in. Sit."

Garrett dropped the folder on her desk. "I have conditions," he said.

She leaned back in her chair and removed her reading glasses. Two tiny parakeets fluttered in a large cage behind her. A small smile played over her lips. "I'm listening."

CHAPTER TWO

SPECIAL AGENT CLAIRE DAWSON had spent five years hunting predators. She refused to become prey.

The three women staring back at her from the computer screen hadn't had a choice. Sarah Mitchell, thirty-one. Rebecca Torres, twenty-eight. Amanda Greenwood, thirty-three. All brunetts. All with careers in law enforcement or victim advocacy. All dead within a week of receiving their stalker's first direct message.

Claire's own FBI photo sat in the fourth position on her screen.

She leaned back in her desk chair, the squeak of worn leather loud in the nearly empty office. She was the only agent still at her desk in the Behavioral Analysis Unit. The fluorescent lights hummed overhead, casting everything in that particular shade of institutional white that made late nights feel even longer.

Her coffee had gone cold an hour ago. She didn't care.

The pattern was there. She could feel it, just out of reach. Something that connected these women beyond the obvious similarities. Something the stalker saw that made them targets.

Survivors. They were all survivors.

Sarah Mitchell had escaped an abusive relationship. Rebecca Torres had fought off a carjacker. Amanda Greenwood had been sexually assaulted in college and testified against her attacker.

And Claire... Claire had survived the night Lily died.

Her hand moved unconsciously to the scar on her left forearm. Fifteen years healed, barely visible now, but she felt it every time she worked a case like this. Felt the break, the cast, the helplessness of being fourteen with a concussion while police asked her what happened to her best friend.

I tried to fight him. Lily told me to run. I should have stayed.

Her phone buzzed.

Claire glanced at the screen, expecting another update from the protection detail that had been shadowing her for the past three days. Instead, an unknown number. A text message that made ice slide down her spine.

Day 3, Claire. Your friend couldn't outrun him. Will you?

Her hands shook as she screenshotted the message, forwarded it to the case team, and documented the timestamp. Calm and controlled. Never mind that her heart was trying to hammer its way out of her chest.

Three days since the first direct message. According to the pattern, she had four days left. Maybe five if she was lucky.

The intercom on her desk crackled. "Dawson. My office. Now."

SAC Marcus Reeves didn't wait for acknowledgment before the line went dead.

Claire stood, checked her weapon out of habit, and walked down the hallway. She tried not to feel like she was walking to her own execution.

Reeves looked like he'd aged five years in the past week. The Special Agent in Charge of the BAU was in his fifties, a former profiler himself, with the kind of experience that made agents feel safe under his command.

Right now, he looked exhausted. "Sit," he said.

Claire remained standing. "Sir, I just received—"

"I know." He turned his computer screen toward her. The exact text she'd received, along with metadata that made her stomach drop. "He accessed our internal network. Again. Third breach in forty-eight hours."

"Then we need to find out how—"

"You're off the case."

The words hit like a physical blow. She stammered, snapped her mouth shut, and tried again. "Sir, I—"

"Effective immediately." Reeves stood, came around his desk. "You're compromised, Claire. This isn't a discussion."

"But I'm the best person to work this case." She fought to keep her voice level. "I know his pattern better than anyone. I've studied these victims for weeks."

"You're not studying victims anymore. You *are* the victim." His voice was gentle but firm. "And victims don't work their own cases."

The hell I'm a victim. "I'm an FBI agent."

"Being stalked by a serial killer." Reeves pulled up another file, this one of security footage. A man's silhouette stood outside her apartment building. Timestamp: *Wednesday, 6:43 PM.* "He was at your building. We have multiple sightings in the past week."

Claire stared at the screen. She'd felt watched. Dismissed it as paranoia.

"There's more." Reeves showed her another photo. A package, addressed to her, that had been intercepted at the FBI mailroom screening. Inside was a bracelet. Silver, delicate.

Exactly like the one Lily had worn. The one that was buried with her.

"How did he—"

"We don't know. But he seems to know things about you, Claire. Personal things. Things from before you were an agent." Reeves met her eyes. "This isn't random. Our team believes he's been planning this for a long time."

The team? Had her unit been talking to him behind her back?

She wanted to argue. Wanted to insist she could handle it, that she'd trained for this, that running wouldn't solve anything. But the bracelet sat in that evidence bag like an accusation.

Her voice came out a touch too shaky. "What's the... plan?"

"We're sending you to a secure location in Montana. Private security contractor with former Special Forces experience. You'll be protected while we work the case."

"*Montana?*" The word came out sharp, harsh. "You're sending me across the country to hide in a safe house while everyone else hunts him?"

"He's here, in D.C. You need to be somewhere he can't reach."

"A safe house here makes sense. Montana is exile."

"Montana is remote, defensible, and off any radar he might have access to." Reeves's voice hardened slightly. "This *predator* has breached FBI security three times." The media had dubbed him the Countdown Killer. While no one on her team was allowed to refer to him that way, she knew they all did in their minds, even Reeves. "He knows where you live, where you work. Your running route, your coffee shop, your dry cleaner."

Claire's jaw clenched. "So we're giving him what he wants—me off the case."

"We're keeping you alive long enough to catch him."

"I should be *here*." Her voice cracked despite her best efforts. "Working this."

"You're too close." Reeves softened slightly. "I know why you do this work, Claire. I know about Lily Harper."

Claire's stomach dropped. "That's in my sealed psych eval."

"I'm your SAC, and it's hardly top secret information. It was all over the news back then." He paused. "I've seen it before. You became an agent to catch men like the one who killed your best friend. You've done good work. Important work. But right now, your job is to stay alive."

"While other agents work *my* case."

"Yes." No apology in it. Just fact. "We have a full team on this. Good agents. They'll find him."

Claire looked away, fighting the burn behind her eyes. Five years of hunting predators. Every arrest for Lily. Every case closed because she wouldn't let another family go through what hers had.

And now she was the victim.

"The contractor is Shadow Point Security," Reeves continued. "They specialize in high-risk protection."

"I don't need a babysitter."

"I won't trust your life with anyone but the best." Reeves shuffled several folders on the desk. "Their team leader is a former SEAL Commander, and I'm assured you'll be in good hands."

Great, a former SEAL. She'd worked with Special Forces before. They were more than competent but tended to treat civilians—even FBI agents—like fragile cargo. "When do I leave?"

"Tonight. A car's waiting downstairs." He must have

seen the protest forming. "That's an order, Agent Dawson."

She stood there, hands clenched at her sides, every instinct screaming to fight this. But orders were orders.

"Can I at least work the case remotely?"

Reeves paused. "I'll keep you in the loop. You can review the case materials and provide input on the profile. But only from the Shadow Point compound, secure channels only." His voice hardened. "If you compromise your location or security in any way, I will pull you completely. Understood?"

"Yes, sir."

"Good. Shadow Point's contact information has been sent in an encrypted email. They'll brief you on arrival."

Claire turned to leave.

"Claire." Reeves's voice stopped her at the door. "We'll catch him."

She looked back. "Without me, it seems."

"Just promise you'll stay alive long enough for us to do it. Don't make me attend your funeral. That's an order."

The words hung in the air. Claire nodded once and walked out.

She always kept a go-bag in her office. Along with that, she grabbed her laptop, case files, and the photograph she kept in her desk drawer of her and Lily as young girls, laughing at something long forgotten.

Before everything changed.

The black SUV was waiting where Reeves said it would be. Professional driver, silent and efficient. Claire climbed into the back seat and stared out the window as D.C. rolled past in the darkness.

She should stay, hunt this bastard, not run off to Montana.

But the memory came anyway. Always did when she thought about Lily.

The hospital. Her broken arm, a concussion, and her parents crying in the hallway. The detective asking what happened.

"He took Lily. I tried to stop him. She told me to run. I should have stayed. I should have—"

"You did what you could, sweetheart. You survived."

But Lily hadn't.

Claire pulled out her phone, opened the case file she'd copied to her secure drive. Three victims. Three dead women who looked like her, who'd survived violence before, who'd fought back.

He was choosing survivors. Testing if they could survive again.

Proving they couldn't.

Not me, Claire thought. *I won't be number four.*

The private airstrip was small, the plane smaller. Claire slept maybe an hour on the flight, dreams full of Lily and bracelets and men's silhouettes in doorways.

The flight took longer than she anticipated, as a storm over the Midwest diverted the plane south before it could resume its flight path. When she landed, dawn was breaking over mountains that seemed impossibly vast compared to the urban land-scape she'd left behind. A different driver, same silent professionalism, drove her through a small town called Blackridge.

Main Street. The Last Stand bar. Local diner. Post office.

Quaint. Normal. The kind of place where everyone knew everyone.

Claire had never felt more exposed in her life.

The compound sat outside town, tucked against the mountains. From the road, it looked like nondescript buildings, a parking area, and modest, generic signage that didn't disclose its true identity.

Up close, Claire's trained eye caught the details. Cameras on every angle. Reinforced doors. Electronic locks. Defensive positioning.

This wasn't just a safe house. This was a tactical installation.

A woman waited at the entrance. Mid-thirties, dark hair, intelligent eyes. "Agent Dawson. Welcome. I'm Dr. Genevieve Montgomery. Call me Vivi." Her voice was cultured. "I'm sorry for the circumstances."

"Yeah, me, too. When do I meet my protection detail?" Claire kept her voice professional, but she was exhausted, frustrated, and in no mood for small talk.

"This morning. First, let's get you settled." Dr. Montgomery led her inside, down a hallway to a room that looked more like a decent hotel than a prison cell. "You'll have access to secure internet for your work. Our communications are encrypted."

Claire dropped her bag on the bed, turned to face the doctor. "Who exactly are you people?"

"We're specialists who handle threats law enforcement can't neutralize quickly enough." Dr. Montgomery's smile was slight. "Your job here is to stay safe while the FBI works your case."

"My job is to catch predators, not hide from them."

"You don't like being sidelined."

"Would you?"

Dr. Montgomery studied her for a moment. "I've reviewed your file. Your work on the Riverside Strangler case was impressive. Your profile led to his arrest."

Claire didn't respond. It had been her first big case. More had followed.

"The FBI's behavioral analysis on your stalker is...adequate," Dr. Montgomery continued, "but I think we can do better."

Claire's attention sharpened. "What do you mean?"

"I've developed a new profiling methodology that combines traditional behavioral analysis with neuropsychological markers and predictive modeling." She pulled out a tablet and showed Claire a complex flowchart. "It's called Trident Therapy. Three-pronged approach—behavioral, neurological, environmental."

"I've never heard of it."

"The Bureau doesn't have access to it. But I've used it with operatives for years. It's designed to help them understand themselves and their enemies on a deeper level. I believe with a few modifications, it can help us understand predators and serial killers, too."

Claire moved closer to the screen, studying it. The

tool was sophisticated. More comprehensive than standard FBI profiling protocols...but was it accurate?

"Traditional profiling tells us a lot about the suspect's personality and habits," Montgomery went on, "helping us understand behaviors and potential patterns. My work takes that to a more analytical level. I don't like educated guesses. I like solid facts that lead to better options."

"You want to re-profile my stalker."

"I want *us* to re-profile him. Together." Dr. Montgomery met her eyes. "Fresh perspective, new methodology, no preconceptions from the FBI's work. You know this case better than anyone. I have tools you don't. Working as a team, perhaps we can uncover this killer's next move."

Claire hesitated. "But *my* team is already working the case."

"We're not interfering with their agenda or procedures. You're consulting, independently." A pause. "Anything we discover, you can share with them. Or...if we find an imminent threat you feel is important, we can act on it first and loop them in when you're ready."

That was bending the rules. Claire knew it. But the alternative was sitting here on the sidelines while other agents hunted *her* predator. "What makes your methodology different?"

"Your stalker chose you specifically. You're his type. But from what I've learned, there's a psychological architecture to his obsession." Dr. Montgomery pulled up another screen. "These women,"—she gestured to the three victims—"were all survivors. But so are thousands of other women. They resemble you, but again, so do hundreds of other women. Why these three? Why you?"

"The FBI profilers already established—"

"They established demographics, opportunity, and general behavioral patterns." Dr. Montgomery's voice was patient but firm. "I'm talking about the specific psychological framework that made him choose you. Not just any survivor. *You*, Claire."

Claire stared at the screen. The same question had nagged at her for weeks.

"He's been watching you for how long?" Dr. Montgomery asked. "Weeks, possibly months?"

"That we know of."

"What if it's been longer? What if he's been building toward this since...Lily's death?"

Claire's chest refused to expand. The bracelet flashed through her mind. "You've done your research."

Dr. Montgomery's voice was gentle now. "He targets survivors—women who fought back and lived. You survived what happened to Lily. Were those other women's deaths simply a lead-up to yours? Are you the true target? Are you unfinished business to him?"

Claire's throat was tight. "You sound as if you're suggesting it's the same killer. Lily's killer is dead."

"And you're still here. Still fighting his kind. I don't think he's the same man, but he might have a tie to him. Worship him. Want to be like him. Or it could be that he simply hates that you hunt serial killers. That's what he wants to take from you."

Fighting back the emotions, the memories threatening to cap her at the knees, she cleared her throat. "When do we start?" The question came out before she could second-guess it.

"This afternoon? After you get some rest."

"I don't need rest. I need to work."

Dr. Montgomery smiled slightly. "I can see why your SAC respects you. All right. Let me set up the system. Two hours?"

"Yes."

After she left, Claire unpacked methodically. Laptop on the desk. Case files organized. Weapon cleaned and loaded, set on the nightstand. Beside it, the photo of her and Lily.

She changed into jeans and a comfortable button-down shirt, keeping her FBI credentials and badge visible on her belt. A reminder that she was an agent, not a victim.

The window offered a view of the mountains, vast and beautiful, and slightly overwhelming to her urban senses. Reinforced glass, she noted. Nothing got through these windows.

Claire pulled up the case files on her laptop. Studied the messages again.

Day 3, Claire. Your friend couldn't outrun him. Will you?

He knew about Lily. Knew what happened. Had he known Lily's killer? Was this connected somehow?

Her phone buzzed with a text from Reeves: *Team is en route to interview potential suspect. Will update.*

Her pulse sped up. She almost texted back,

demanding to be included in the interview, but stopped herself.

She was in Montana. Hidden. Safe.

Useless.

No. Not useless. She had Dr. Montgomery's Trident methodology. She had five years of experience. She had every file, every message, every piece of evidence.

She'd find him from here if she had to.

Her inbox chimed with an internal email from Dr. Montgomery. Claire pulled up the flowchart, started reading about neuropsychological markers and predictive behavioral modeling. It was fascinating. More sophisticated than anything she'd seen at the Bureau. Her mind soaked it up, reading and rereading. She scribbled notes. Wished she had coffee.

Her lids dipped half a dozen times. She pushed herself to stay awake and keep circling different ideas. If this worked—if she and Montgomery could identify the killer before the FBI did—

There was a knock at her door.

Claire glanced at the clock. Ten thirty. Three hours had passed without her noticing.

"Agent Dawson? Your briefing is ready."

A male voice. Deep, controlled. The kind of voice that came from years of command.

Claire took a breath, cleared her mind, and opened the door.

The man in the hallway stood at attention. Former military was written in every line of his posture. "Agent

Dawson." His voice was professional, carefully neutral. "I'll show you to the conference room."

"Are you my bodyguard?"

His lips quirked. "That would be Wolf. He's busy at the moment, designing your security protocols and getting the team up to speed on you."

"Wolf?" It came out in a huff, part disbelief and part confusion. "That's his name?"

"His call sign, ma'am. We all use them."

Call sign, right. They used codenames for themselves and probably would for her and the mission. "And you are?"

"Lynx."

"What's mine?"

He lifted a brow, looked slightly uncomfortable. "Ma'am?"

"You may be ex-Special Forces, but you act like Secret Service, right? You've already given me a call sign, haven't you? Like JFK was Lancer. Nixon was Passkey. Carter was Rawhide. What's mine?"

His gaze dropped to his boots. "Uh, that's something you should discuss with Wolf."

Her curiosity was piqued. "That bad, huh?"

He rolled his lips in as if hiding a grin and gestured down the hallway. "Dr. Montgomery is waiting in the conference room."

Claire followed, the past stirred up in her head, and the present playing mind tricks with her.

They reached the conference room where Dr. Montgomery waited with a tablet and several files. Lynx nodded and left. Nothing personal in any of it.

"Agent Dawson," Dr. Montgomery said. "Let's get started."

Claire took a seat, pulled out her laptop, and forced herself to focus. She was here to work. To hunt. To prove she wasn't prey.

Everything else could wait.

Even the uncomfortable truth that being here made her feel something she hadn't felt in fifteen years.

Safe.

CHAPTER THREE

Garrett had imagined this moment a thousand times in fifteen years. None of his scenarios involved Claire failing to recognize him.

He stood outside her door, hand raised to knock, heart pounding in a way that had nothing to do with tactical operations and everything to do with the four-teen-year-old girl who'd cried at his sister's grave.

She's not fourteen anymore. She's an FBI agent. A woman who hunts the same monsters that killed Lily.

And she had no idea Bobby Anderson was about to walk back into her life.

He'd spent the night going over his conditions with the doctor and strategizing his team. The list was short but non-negotiable: Montgomery wasn't to share that he was Bobby, Lily's brother.

He was a completely different person now than the kid Claire had met only three, maybe four times growing up. His and Lily's mom had remarried and moved to

D.C., leaving him and his dad behind. Garrett had lived with their father, mostly because he'd always been a handful, and Stephanie, their mom, hadn't been able to keep him in check. He looked and talked differently now. Hell, he even thought differently. The Navy had cleaned him up after he'd spiraled because of Lily's death and given him purpose. It was crucial to him that the past stayed buried where it belonged.

Vivi had agreed. For now.

She'd also given him free rein in picking his team for this assignment. Operation Paperclip was no different from the missions he'd led in the field. He'd picked his team based on their strengths—surveillance, perimeter defense, overwatch—and built a layered security bubble to keep Claire safe.

She'd spent the morning with the doctor, learning the Trident system and how Vivi was adapting it to hunt predators. Now, he couldn't put it off any longer—he had to face the music. He had to face *her*.

Garrett knocked, letting his professional operator face slide into place. "Agent Dawson? Your briefing is ready."

The door opened.

Time stopped.

Fifteen years collapsed into nothing. Those blue eyes —Lily's best friend's eyes, the ones that had looked at him with such guilt at the funeral—met his. But they were different now. Harder. Older. Scarred by what she'd survived and the things she'd witnessed since.

She was beautiful. Not the skinny fourteen-year-old

with a broken arm, but a woman who'd turned her trauma into purpose.

Lily would have been proud.

"Agent Dawson." He kept his voice carefully neutral. "I'm Wolf. We need to discuss your security protocols."

She blinked. Studied his face with an intensity that made his pulse spike. FBI training, he told himself. She assessed everyone like this.

But her eyes lingered. On his jaw. His eyes. The set of his shoulders.

"Wolf, right." She smirked. "Did you pick that yourself or just draw the short straw?"

Was she teasing? "Operational callsign. Everyone here uses them for their safety and yours." He gestured down the hallway. "Dr. Montgomery is waiting in the conference room."

"And believe it or not, I can find it on my own. I spent the morning there."

"Please refrain from going anywhere unattended, Agent Dawson."

"It's Claire, and does that include the bathroom, Wolf?"

The sarcasm could peel paint. He started walking, hiding his grin. "The building is a security facility, but I want eyes on you at all times." He held up a hand when she started to protest. "Bathroom trips excluded."

She made a sound of frustration as she followed him down the hallway, and Garrett was hyperaware of every move, every sound she made. The cadence and quiet efficiency of her footsteps. The jut of her chin. The fall of her hair over her shoulder when she turned to look at him.

"How long have you worked here?" she asked.

Damn, that voice. So smooth and sexy. *Stay professional. She's a protectee. Nothing more.*

But his hands were shaking.

"How long have you been with Shadow Point?" she asked again. The question was more pointed this time, analytical. She was gathering intelligence.

"I'm the first tactical commander."

"You're avoiding my question." She stopped abruptly. "This is a new operation, isn't it? Am I your first guinea pig?"

Damn, she was good. "We're a new unit that's part of an established organization offering personal security for years. Shadow Point specifically handles stalkers and serial killers." He glanced at her, gestured for her to start walking again. "I assure you, you're in good hands."

She was quiet for a moment. "Have we met before? You seem..."

Garrett's heart stopped.

He turned to face her, forcing himself to meet those blue eyes. "I've been deployed for most of the past fifteen years."

"Maybe at a joint task force briefing? I've worked with SEALs before."

"We all blend together, don't we? At least, that's our goal." He winked, making a joke. Once again, he motioned her forward. "Shall we?"

She frowned, but she let it drop.

Garrett released a mental sigh of relief, trying not to think about how close she was. How, after fifteen years of wondering if CJ was okay, she was here. Alive. Strong. Everything he'd hoped she'd become.

And so far, she hadn't recognized him.

The conference room was all business. Vivi sat at the head of the table with files, a tablet, and three cups of coffee. She'd set up tactical displays on the wall screens— maps, timelines, victim photos.

"Agent Dawson." Vivi's voice was warm. "Wolf will brief you on security protocols, and then we can begin our profiling work."

Claire sat, pulled out her laptop. "He already did— don't go anywhere without a bodyguard." She fixed him with a glare. "Look, I appreciate the protection, but I'm here to work. Dr. Montgomery and I will be re-profiling my stalker using her Trident methodology."

"Understood." Garrett leaned against the wall, arms crossed. "My job is to keep you alive while you do that."

"I don't need a babysitter."

He held her glare. "I'm a tactical operator with fifteen years of experience hunting predators in hostile environments. You're a high-value target with a serial killer fixated on you. That makes this a protection operation, not babysitting."

Her eyes narrowed. Alpha recognizing alpha. "I'm not some civilian."

"No. You're an FBI agent with five years of field experience." He kept his voice even. "Which means you know how dangerous your stalker is. You've seen what he did to three women who looked exactly like you."

That hit home. Her jaw tightened.

Vivi intervened smoothly. "Perhaps we should move on to the threat assessment?"

She pulled up the case file on the main screen. Three victim photos: Sarah Mitchell. Rebecca Torres. Amanda Greenwood. Her notes listed the obvious—they were all dark-haired, blue-eyed, with similar cheekbones, noses, and lips. Just like Claire.

But they were all dead.

"The timeline from first direct message to death ranges from five to seven days," Vivi said. "Agent Dawson received her first direct message four days ago."

Garrett's stomach went cold. He already knew it, but hearing it again set that countdown clock in his head all over again. Four days. She had one, maybe three, left.

Except now, she had him.

No one was coming through his protection. *No one.*

"How did he breach FBI security?" he asked.

"Unknown." Vivi pulled up technical reports. "He's accessed their internal network three times. Either he's inside the Bureau or has compromised someone who is."

Claire looked sick at the thought. "Everyone on my team has been thoroughly vetted."

"It could be anyone," Garrett said, "from the mailroom attendant to the janitor. And vetted doesn't mean they're above being bribed or blackmailed." He eyed the photos of the dead women staring back at him. "The previous victims—where were they when he struck?"

"Two were at home. One in a parking garage at her workplace." Vivi shifted the screen to crime scene photos. The graphic nature was tough to look at. "It appears that he learns their patterns and strikes when they're most vulnerable. Not unusual for this type of serial killer."

Garrett studied the photos with the cold assessment of someone who'd hunted men like this. "He's patient. Organized. This isn't about rage. It's about control."

"Yes." Claire's voice was quiet. "He targets survivors. Women who fought abusers and stalkers and lived."

"Agent Dawson survived an attack fifteen years ago," Vivi said gently, giving him a pointed look.

The words hung in the air.

Garrett's hand tightened on his arm. *Don't react. Don't let her see you know.*

But Vivi continued to stare, saying nothing else. Giving him an opening. The psychologist in her hadn't been happy about him wanting to keep it a secret. She'd told him that disassociating from his younger self wasn't healthy.

To him, it seemed like the healthiest decision he'd ever made.

Claire focused on her screen, sharing the profile she'd been building on the main one. "He's not just killing to satisfy some primal urge. He's proving a point."

"Which is?" Garrett asked, even though he already knew.

"These women survived once. He's showing them— showing everyone—that they're not as strong as they think they are." Her voice was clinical, detached. "It's about correcting what he sees as failures. Women who should have died but didn't."

He held in the anger rushing through his veins. "He's punishing them for surviving?"

Claire looked at him. Really looked. Something shifted in her expression. Recognition, but not the kind he feared. Understanding. "Yes. Exactly."

For a moment, they just stared at each other. Two people who understood what it meant to hunt monsters. Who knew the weight of survivor's guilt.

Then Garrett looked away.

"Or," Vivi said. "The three women are proof that he can control things. He could be trying to prove to Claire specifically that he has the cunning and smarts to deliver justice. That he can outsmart her and the FBI. It's personal to him, and he wants Claire to be scared. To fear him."

Garrett dropped his hands to his sides. Fisted them. "Agent Dawson, we need to discuss security protocols."

She didn't argue, sitting back and nodding. But the next twenty minutes were a negotiation, anyway. She pushed back on every restriction. Garrett held firm on most of them.

"You don't leave the compound without me," he said.

"I'm not a prisoner."

"You're a target. There's a difference."

"I'm in Montana. He's in D.C."

"You can't let your guard down."

He laid out the rest of the rules. No outside communication except through secure channels. Check-ins every two hours if they weren't in the same room. A guard would be posted outside her quarters at all times.

He pulled out a tracking unit the size of a nail head. "I need to attach this to your shoe. In fact, I need your entire wardrobe."

She looked scandalized. "For what?"

"First, to make sure you don't have any trackers on you, and secondly, to attach ours in case the worst-case scenario happens and you go missing."

"You're kidding, right?"

He stared at her, stone cold.

Her hands flew up, and she rolled her eyes. "These protocols are excessive and restrictive."

"Three women are dead. Excessive and restrictive are appropriate."

"The stalker doesn't know I'm here."

Garrett leaned forward. "You sure about that?"

That stopped her. She wasn't sure—he could see it in her eyes. If there was a breach at the FBI, the killer might know she was here.

The briefest flicker of fear flashed across her face. He felt like a dick.

As he walked to her and gestured for her to give him her shoe, he softened his voice. "Work with Dr. Montgomery on the profile. I'll coordinate with your SAC on any leads. You want to hunt the Countdown Killer? Fine. But we do it smart."

Claire studied him for a long moment, slipping her shoe back on when he handed it to her. "You've done this before."

"I've protected high-value targets in hostile environments. You're no different."

"Flattering."

"Wasn't meant to be." The corner of his mouth almost twitched.

Vivi stood. "Wolf, perhaps you could show Agent Dawson the compound security features and get her some lunch? We can regroup at two."

Claire nodded. "Sounds good." She started packing up her computer, then stopped and stretched. Sighed. "Lead the way, Wolf."

The codename felt like armor. Safe. She couldn't trace Wolf to Bobby. Couldn't connect the dots between her new bodyguard's callsign and an eighteen-year-old kid at his sister's funeral.

But every time she said it, something in his chest tightened.

The compound tour took them through the building's three levels. Garrett showed her the command center with its wall of monitors and secure communications. The armory, which made her eyebrows rise slightly—impressive even by FBI standards. The training facility where he'd been running drills since dawn, trying to work off the nervous energy of knowing he'd see her today. It had also given him time with his team—Lynx, Grizzly, and Hawk—to brief them on the assignment.

"It's quite impressive," she observed.

"This team is made up of people who understand how to hunt predators outside the system. Lynx handles our surveillance and cyber security—if the Countdown

Killer tries to track you digitally, he'll know. Grizzly manages perimeter defense and close protection. Hawk provides overwatch and long-range reconnaissance. Between the four of us and Dr. Montgomery's psychological expertise, you're covered from every angle."

"Vigilantes."

"Operators who get results when bureaucracy gets in the way." He glanced at her. "You became an FBI agent to catch killers. Sometimes the system isn't fast enough."

"The system has rules for a reason."

"The system is supposed to protect the innocent. Sometimes it protects the guilty." He stopped walking and turned to face her. "Everyone here has been burned. Each operator—even the doctor—is motivated to stop predators from hurting the innocent. You can call us whatever you want, but if you heard our stories, you'd understand."

Her jaw tightened. Point made.

They ended up outside, overlooking the mountains. The September day was cool and clear. The vast Montana landscape spread out before them, mighty and indifferent.

"It's beautiful here," Claire said quietly.

"Different from D.C."

"Everything's different from D.C." She wrapped her arms around herself. "I should be there. Working my case."

"You are working it. Just from here."

"While other agents do the actual investigating."

Garrett studied her profile. The frustration. The

helplessness. He knew that feeling. Had lived it for eighteen months, drinking himself into numbness in Montana because he couldn't fix what he'd broken in Colombia.

"Your job is to stay alive long enough to see him caught," he said.

"That's what my SAC said."

"Smart man."

She looked at him then. Those blue eyes that saw too much. "Why do you care?"

Because I promised your best friend I'd take care of you. Because I failed once and won't fail again. Because you're CJ and I'm Bobby and fifteen years hasn't changed that.

"It's my job," he said.

"Feels like more than that. Like you have one of those stories that gives you the motivation to help me."

It was so much more than that. But he couldn't tell her. Wouldn't. It would change their dynamic too much.

"Let's get you some food, Agent Dawson."

"Claire." Her voice was softer. "You can call me Claire."

The name felt wrong in his mouth. She was CJ. Would always be CJ to him.

"Claire," he said.

She smiled slightly. "Thank you for the tour. And for..." She gestured vaguely. "All of this."

He held the door to return inside.

"So what's my call sign?"

He stopped in his tracks. "Excuse me?"

She smiled a cunning, devious little smile. "My call

sign. I know I have one. Lynx wouldn't tell me. Said I had to ask you."

Shit. "My unit will address you as Agent Dawson."

"To my face, yes," she said, still smiling. "Come on. We're professionals here. What embarrassing call sign did you give me?"

This was going to go all kinds of wrong. The gleam in her eyes told him she wouldn't quit until she'd weaseled it out of him or one of the others. Knowing Vivi, she'd probably tell her. "Paperclip."

Claire's jaw dropped open. "Come again."

He mashed his lips together. Took a fortifying mental breath. "Your call sign is Paperclip."

The smile morphed into a look of disgust. "Paperclip," she echoed, realization dawning. "Because you think of me as a desk jockey?"

Yep, his life was about to become a living hell over a stupid name. "The victims all look like you. You're the hinge—the paperclip—that brings the case together."

She paced away, came back. He knew she was gearing up for more, but she surprised him when she said, "The stalker sent me a bracelet." Her voice was quiet now. Vulnerable. "Silver. Delicate. My best friend had one just like it when we were girls. She was taken, killed. The man took me, too, but I survived."

Garrett's chest constricted. Lily's bracelet. *The one we buried with her.*

"She was murdered fifteen years ago," Claire continued, not realizing he already knew. "It's why I do this work. Catching men like the Countdown Killer."

He should say something. Anything. But his throat was tight. "I'm sorry," he managed.

Claire's eyes were distant, lost in memories. "That's why he's chosen me, because I'm some sort of unfinished business. The one who got away."

Garrett took a step toward her. Couldn't help it. "You fought back and lived. That took strength. Now, you suffer from survivor's guilt and a need for vengeance."

She looked at him, surprise in her expression. "You sound like the doctor."

He shrugged. "She's rubbed off on me. What can I say?"

"Do you suffer from survivor's guilt and a need for vengeance, too?"

She had no idea. "I lost someone." The words came out before he could stop them. "A long time ago."

He didn't elaborate. Couldn't. Every word was a minefield.

"I get it—this is why you're here. The story that turned you into..." She gestured at him. "Wolf."

They stood there in the cool Montana air, two people connected by grief they couldn't share. Survivors of violence that had shaped everything they'd become.

Claire's voice was barely a whisper. "Her name was Lily."

The name hit him like a fist to the chest. He nodded. Didn't trust his voice.

After a moment, she turned back for the door. "I think I'll skip lunch."

"Yeah."

He watched her walk away, this woman who'd been a girl at his sister's grave. Who'd become an FBI agent to hunt the kind of monster who'd killed Lily. Who had no idea Bobby Anderson was standing right here, watching her like he could keep her safe through sheer force of will.

I'm here, Lil. I'm protecting her like I should have protected you.

THE REST of the day passed in controlled chaos. Claire worked with Vivi on the Trident methodology, diving deep into behavioral markers and neurological patterns. Garrett coordinated with the FBI, including SAC Reeves, on security updates and case developments. He reviewed the compound's defensive positions, reviewed files on additional operators for future assignments, and tried not to think about Claire three rooms away.

Failed on that last count.

Dinner was in the compound mess. Claire and Vivi sat at one table, Garrett and his team at another. All three of his teammates were sharp, had good ideas, and were as focused as he was on keeping the compound and Claire safe.

After dinner, Garrett escorted Claire to her room.

"I know you think I'm difficult," she said as they reached her door.

"I think you're scared and trying not to show it."

She stiffened. "I'm not—"

"You should be." He softened his voice. "He's killed

three women. You're next on his list. Being scared doesn't make you weak. It makes you smart."

Claire studied him and nodded. "Thank you. I appreciate what you're doing, although we're going to discuss changing my call sign tomorrow."

There was that small smile again. He should walk away. Maintain distance. But her eyes held him there.

Lynx showed up for guard duty.

Garrett cleared his throat. "Get some rest, Claire."

"Goodnight, Wolf."

He nodded and walked away before he said something he couldn't take back.

His quarters were Spartan. Bed, desk, bathroom. He'd unpacked his go-bag but hadn't bothered to make the space personal. Wasn't planning to stay long-term. Just until Claire was safe.

Then what? Back to drinking in The Last Stand? Back to hiding?

He sat on the edge of the bed, head in his hands.

I saw her. I talked to her. She doesn't know who I am.

Relief and grief warred in his chest.

His secure phone buzzed. FBI. "Wolf," he answered.

"Commander, it's SAC Reeves. We have a development."

Garrett sat up straighter. "What kind of development?"

"A potential suspect. We arrested him tonight in D.C. on unrelated charges—possession with intent to distribute. White male, late thirties, fits the profile. He lives in Agent Dawson's apartment building. There are photos of her in his place."

Garrett's heart pounded. "Is it him?"

"Too early to tell. We're bringing him in for questioning. Running his background, checking his movements against the timeline." Reeves paused. "If it's him, Agent Dawson can come home, but I haven't shared this with her yet. I don't want to get her hopes up until I have solid proof."

Home. Away from here. *Away from me.*

That's what Garrett should want—her safe. The threat eliminated.

But his chest was tight.

"Something feels off, though," Reeves continued. "It's too easy. This predator has been meticulous. He wouldn't leave photos lying around where we could find them."

"Could be a mistake. They make them."

"Maybe." But Reeves didn't sound convinced. "Keep Agent Dawson secured. I'll update you as soon as I can after the interview."

The line went dead.

Garrett sat in the darkness, processing.

If it was the stalker, Claire left and went back to D.C. Back to her life.

If it wasn't, she stayed in danger, but with him.

He should pray it was the stalker. Should want this over. But part of him—the part that was still Bobby, that had never stopped being Bobby—wanted her to stay.

What the hell is wrong with me?

His phone buzzed again. Text message.

Claire: *Can't sleep. You awake?*

Garrett stared at the screen.

He shouldn't respond. Should maintain professional distance. She was a protectee. He was her operator. Nothing more.

His thumb moved before his brain caught up. *Yeah. What do you need?*

Three dots. She was typing.

Garrett waited, torn between the kid who'd failed his sister and the man who'd learned to hunt monsters. Between Bobby's promise and Wolf's mission. Between keeping Claire safe and keeping her at a distance.

Her message came through: *Tell me about being a SEAL. What was it like?*

She wanted to understand him. To know who he was behind the callsign.

And that was the most dangerous thing of all.

CHAPTER FOUR

Claire stared at her phone screen, watching the three dots appear, disappear, then appear again.

She'd asked Wolf what it was like to be a SEAL. Simple question. The kind of small talk people made when they couldn't sleep and were texting someone they barely knew but somehow felt comfortable reaching out to.

His response finally came through. *The Navy gave me purpose. Structure.*

She read it twice. Short. Controlled. The kind of answer designed to give information without actually revealing anything.

Claire dug some more. *What was your favorite mission?*

The three dots took longer this time. She imagined him lying in bed somewhere in this compound, choosing his words carefully.

Can't talk about most of them. Classified.

Fair enough. Still, there had to be *something* he could share.

Why did you get out?

Another long pause. The three dots appeared and disappeared three times before his response came through.

Went off mission. Command didn't appreciate it.

Claire sat up straighter in bed. That wasn't the standard 'medical discharge' or 'completed my service' answer. That was an admission of something. Someone who'd broken rules, crossed lines. Done something his superiors couldn't officially sanction.

Her profiler brain kicked into gear. Wolf had gone off-mission—unauthorized action. Gotten caught or suspected, and discharged for it, hadn't he?

But he was here now, running security for Shadow Point, a company that operated in the gray areas law enforcement couldn't reach.

What kind of mission? she typed.

No dots this time.

She waited a full minute. Nothing.

I know you didn't fall asleep, Wolf. If you can't talk about it, that's okay. What can you talk about?

Still, he didn't answer.

Not directly anyway. In some ways, it confirmed exactly what she thought.

Fine. Texts were impersonal and too easy to misinterpret. And he probably didn't trust anyone enough to say more on an app.

Claire looked at her phone, then at her door, then back at her phone.

This was stupid. She should try to sleep. Morning would come early, and she had profiling work to do with Dr. Montgomery.

But she was wide awake now, and more curious about Wolf than she had any right to be.

Before she could second-guess herself, she typed: *Any chance there's tea in this fancy compound of yours?*

She hit send and immediately regretted it. Was she too forward? Too...something.

The three dots appeared almost instantly.

Cafeteria. Give me two minutes. I'll come get you.

Claire exhaled. Okay then.

She got out of bed, traded her pajamas for yoga pants, and put on her FBI Academy sweatshirt. Ran her fingers through her hair—loose around her shoulders instead of pulled back in its usual professional style. Then, she grabbed her phone and headed for the door.

Her hand hesitated on the handle. Was this smart? Trying to force friendship with a man she barely knew in the middle of the night?

Except he wasn't just any man. He was her protection detail, and something about him made her feel...

Safe.

That was the problem, wasn't it? She felt safe with Wolf in a way she hadn't felt safe with anyone in fifteen years.

Claire opened the door.

He stood in the hallway, ten feet away. Grizzly was in full bodyguard mode beside her door.

"Commander," Grizzly said.

"Get some sleep," Wolf replied. "I've got her for tonight."

Then it was just the two of them in the dimly lit corridor. Something about the way he'd said that—*I've got her for tonight*—made Claire's pulse skip.

He wore tactical pants and a black T-shirt that showed off the kind of build a man gained from years of hard training. His hair was slightly mussed, like he'd been lying down. His weapon was holstered at his hip. He still looked professional, but...softer somehow than during the day.

"Agent Dawson." His voice was quiet in the stillness.

"It's after midnight, Wolf. I think we can skip the formalities. Call me Claire."

The corner of his mouth almost twitched. Almost. "This way."

He moved down the hallway with that controlled grace she'd noticed earlier. Always aware. Always assessing. Eyes tracking corners, checking sight lines, never fully relaxed, even in his own compound.

But he slowed his pace for her, keeping just slightly ahead but not so far she'd feel like he was leading her. When they came to the stairs, his hand hovered near her lower back without actually touching it—protective but respectful of her space.

Claire noticed all of it. Filed it away. She told herself

it was a habit—she'd been this way since her encounter with Lily's killer.

Or maybe she was just a woman noticing a man who made her pulse spike.

The cafeteria was industrial but comfortable—stainless steel appliances, long tables, that particular smell of a commercial kitchen. Dim security lighting cast everything in soft shadows.

Wolf moved to a cabinet and pulled it open, revealing an impressive selection of tea. "Chamomile? Earl Grey? Green?" He glanced back at her. "Or do you need something stronger? I think Hawk hides the good stuff somewhere."

"Chamomile's fine. I'd like to sleep eventually."

He pulled down a box, filled an electric kettle with water, and set it to boil. His movements were efficient, economical. He knew exactly where everything was.

Then he opened another cabinet, rummaged for a moment, and emerged with a package of cookies.

"Chocolate chip." He set them on the counter. "Hawk's personal stash, but don't tell him I raided it."

Claire found herself smiling. "Your secret's safe with me."

She watched him work—this man who'd been all tactical assessment and clipped commands during the day was now casually making her tea and stealing cookies. The shift was... surprising.

Appealing.

He caught her staring. "What?"

"Nothing. I didn't peg you for the domestic type."

"I can make tea without burning down a building."
He grabbed two mugs from another cabinet. "Low bar,
but I clear it."

"Impressive résumé."

Was that almost a smile? Hard to tell in the dim light.

The kettle whistled. Wolf poured water over the tea
bags and brought both mugs to the nearest table. He set
the cookies between them and sat down across from her—
close enough to feel intimate, far enough to maintain
distance.

Claire wrapped her hands around the warm mug,
inhaling the faint but familiar scent of chamomile and
honey. "Thank you."

"Can't have my protectee dying of dehydration."

"Pretty sure that's not how dehydration works."

"I'm a SEAL, not a doctor."

There. Definitely almost a smile that time.

Claire took a sip, letting the silence settle. He seemed
comfortable with silence. Another thing she logged into
her mental file on him. "So. Going off mission. What
happened?"

Wolf's expression shuttered. He reached for a cookie
and broke it in half. "What makes you think I'll tell you?"

"Because you're here. You could have told me to go
back to bed."

"You're my protectee. You requested an escort to the
cafeteria for tea. That's my job."

"Right. Your job." She studied him over her mug.
"Except Grizzly was already on night watch. He could
have brought me. You didn't have to relieve him."

Wolf ate half the cookie. Said nothing.

Claire tried a different approach. "You said you went off mission and did something your bosses didn't appreciate. But you also said Shadow Point does the same thing—operates outside official channels when the system's too slow."

"Your point?"

"My point is that you didn't get discharged because you did something wrong. My guess is you got discharged because you did something right that your superiors couldn't officially sanction." She leaned forward slightly. "What was it?"

He was quiet for a long moment. "I don't talk about it."

"Are you ashamed?"

"What?" His expression was a mix of outrage and irritation. "No."

"Is it classified?"

He sighed. "Technically, no. No one knows exactly what I did. There's no record of it, no witnesses."

She mulled that over. "You're just saying that so I won't go digging and find out through my vast and extensive resources. I mean, I have the clearance and the right to investigate anyone who's guarding me, don't I?" Of course, she'd have to learn his real name, but she could if she really wanted to, and they both knew it.

Another sigh. His eyes locked on hers, more irritated now. "On one of my assignments, local women were disappearing from villages near our operational area. Turning up dead. Tortured."

Claire's chest tightened. She set down her tea, hands suddenly shaking. "And?"

"And I tracked the killer. I went off mission for twelve hours. When I came back, the women stopped disappearing." His voice was flat. Emotionless.

"Jesus. You..."

He stared at the half of uneaten cookie. "I won't cop to anything, so don't ask."

"They suspected, didn't they? Your CO? But they must not have had proof, so they discharged you without a court-martial."

"I could have fought it. They didn't have any proof, but I saw the way they looked at me. Like they couldn't trust me anymore. Didn't matter that I'd done an honorable thing."

Her finger slid around the edge of the cup. "You broke the rules. They can't have a SEAL going rogue."

He met her eyes, his hard. "No, not even if going rogue saves lives."

Claire understood. How many times had she wanted to cross lines the FBI wouldn't let her cross? How many predators had she watched walk because of technicalities, jurisdictional issues, bureaucratic delays? "That's why you're here," she said quietly. "Shadow Point. Doing what the system won't let you do."

He continued to study her, but the hardness left his expression. He seemed more...curious. Interested. "Maybe."

She took a sip of tea. "For what it's worth? I think you did the right thing."

His eyes sharpened. "I'm surprised to hear you say that."

She straightened her spine. "Making assumptions about me?"

"Never. Assumptions get people killed."

The temperature between them seemed charged. Anticipatory. Neither said a word. They just...stared at each other.

"Then I'll refrain from making any further ones about you," she said, sneaking his broken cookie.

Wolf was quiet for another moment, then he relaxed slightly and chuckled. "Your assumptions might be accurate. I suspect you're so good at your job that profiling people like me comes easy."

Her cheeks heated at the compliment. Then they heated even more from embarrassment. What was wrong with her? People told her all the time that she was an expert at her job, at profiling. Why did the words coming from him seem to carry so much more weight?

She wanted to ask how he could be so sure she was good at her job. They'd known each other for less than a day. But the moment felt fragile, and she didn't want to break it. "What about before the Navy?" she asked instead. "You have family?"

He tensed again. Sore topic. "Dad was military. He taught me to shoot when I was eight, and he and Mom divorced when I was ten. Mom remarried and moved to D.C. when I was a teenager. I stayed with my dad in Virginia."

"That must have been hard."

"It was what it was."

Deflecting. She recognized the tactic. "Any siblings?"

The pause was too long. His hand tightened around his mug. "A sister," he said finally. "Half-sister, technically. I rarely got to see her."

"Where is she now? Does she live around here?"

His throat worked. He gripped the handle of his mug tighter. "She passed when I was still a teenager."

Claire's chest went tight. She'd meant to create an easy rapport with him, not dredge up bad memories. "I'm so sorry." She knew that pain. Knew what it meant to lose someone young. To spend the rest of your life wondering if you could have saved them. "What was her name?" The question came out before she could stop it.

Wolf's jaw clenched. He cleared his throat and looked away. "What about you?" His voice was rough now. "What made you join the FBI?"

She'd gone too far. He wanted to turn the spotlight off himself. Fair enough.

"My best friend Lily was murdered when we were fourteen. We'd been friends since we were in second grade. She was... everything. Bright, funny, fearless." Claire stared into her tea. "We were walking home from a movie. A man tried to grab both of us. I fought—broke my arm, ended up with a concussion trying to stop him. I got away, but he took her." She drew in a breath, let it out slowly. "They found her three days later."

The words were clinical. Detached. The only way she could say them.

Wolf said nothing, but she sensed his empathy.

"I was useless," she went on. "I couldn't save her. Couldn't even give the police a good description of the guy. The head injury scrambled my memory of his face." She looked up. "So I decided to become someone who could save people. Someone who hunts men like him."

"You were fourteen, and you fought a grown man." Wolf leaned forward. "That's not useless. That's brave."

"I lost her."

"You did what you could." The intensity in his voice caught her off guard. "That matters, Claire."

Something in his voice, the way he said her name—Claire's chest felt too tight.

"Lily would be proud of you," he said.

The certainty in his words stopped her. "But I let her down."

"You were a girl attacked by a monster. You didn't let anyone down."

She pushed the cup away. "Sometimes I wonder if I'm doing this for her or for me."

"Does it matter? You're saving lives either way."

"But am I? Three women are dead. The Countdown Killer is still out there. I'm in Montana drinking tea while—"

"While staying alive and helping your team catch him." Wolf leaned in another inch, close enough that she could see tiny gold flecks in his eyes. "Your job right now is to survive and go on to hunt other killers."

"What if that's not enough?"

"It's everything."

They stared at each other across the table, tea and cookies forgotten. The kitchen felt smaller. Warmer.

Claire was hyperaware of how close he was. The intensity in his gaze. The way his jaw tightened like he was holding himself back from...something. Her eyes dropped to his mouth, just for a second.

His phone buzzed. The spell broke.

He checked his screen. His whole body went rigid.

"What?" Claire asked, instinct driving her to stand. "What is it?"

He didn't answer. He stood and moved to the window with his hand on his weapon.

"Wolf?"

He turned and showed her the screen. A message had come from Lynx. Her body shook as the words registered.

Stalker just posted online. 'Found you, Claire. Montana looks good on you.'

The world tilted. Claire's hands went numb. "He knows." Her voice came from somewhere far away. "He knows I'm here."

Wolf was already moving, radio in hand. "Wolf to all units. Compound lockdown. Paperclip is compromised. I repeat, Paperclip is compromised."

Static crackled. "Lynx here. Copy that."

"Grizzly copies."

"Hawk copies."

Wolf turned to her, all softness gone. This was the operator now. The weapon. "Your room. Now."

Claire moved on shaky legs, rushing beside him down the hallway, her mind racing.

The Countdown Killer had found her. Across the country, in a classified location, with every security measure in place—he'd found her.

How? How was that even possible?

Three women were dead. She was next on his list, and the only thing standing between her and the monster who'd been hunting her was a man she'd known for less than twenty-four hours.

A man who made her feel safer than she had in fifteen years.

A man whose eyes held secrets she couldn't name.

They reached her door. Wolf swept the room—windows, closet, bathroom. Checked locks. Tested window seals.

"Stay here," he said. "Lock the door. Don't open it for anyone but me or Dr. Montgomery. Understand?"

Claire nodded. "He's coming, isn't he? He's going to get me."

Wolf's jaw tightened. His eyes met hers. Steel and stone and something that looked like a promise. "He'll have to go through me first."

CHAPTER FIVE

Garrett gave himself twenty minutes to secure the compound before the Countdown Killer made his next move. Just in case the bastard was actually close by.

The command center was three floors down—monitors covering every angle of the compound, security feeds from perimeter cameras, thermal imaging, motion sensors. Lynx was there when he arrived, fingers flying across keyboards, pulling up data faster than most people could read.

"Show me the post," Garrett said.

Lynx brought up a screenshot on the main screen from a dark web forum. It was timestamped eighteen minutes ago.

Found you, Claire. Montana looks good on you.

Garrett's jaw tightened. The stalker wasn't just taunting her. He was announcing his next move. Trying to make her believe the compound wasn't safe anymore.

"How'd he find her?" Garrett asked.

"Working on it." Lynx didn't look up from his laptop. "But Commander, this location is classified. The only people who knew she was coming here were the Feds and us."

"Then we have a breach. Either in the Bureau or here."

"I'd stake my life it's not here." Lynx pulled up the compound's security logs. "No unauthorized access. No unusual communications. We're clean."

Which meant the leak had to be inside the FBI.

The door opened. Grizzly came in, tactical vest on, weapon loaded. "Perimeter's secure. Hawk's doing a thermal sweep now. You want me on Paperclip's door?"

"No." Garrett moved to the weapons locker and started loading magazines. "I'm with her. You're at the main entrance. No one gets in this building who isn't vetted by me personally."

"Copy that."

The radio crackled. Hawk's voice: "Hawk to Wolf. Perimeter sweep complete. No thermal signatures within five hundred yards. We're clear."

For now.

His blood thrummed with anger. "Understood. Maintain patrol. Report any movement."

"Copy."

He turned back to Lynx. "Pull everything we have on this predator. Geography. Timeline. Methods. I want to know how he operates."

"Already compiled for Dr. Montgomery." Lynx pulled up files. "Agent Dawson has months of research on this guy. She's been hunting him since before he went after her."

Garrett knew that. Which was precisely why he needed her in this briefing, even if every instinct screamed to lock her in her room where nothing could touch her.

The conference room door opened. Claire walked in, dressed in jeans and her FBI sweatshirt, weapon holstered at her hip, credentials clipped to her belt. Not a protectee trying to hide. An agent ready to work and establishing her role with him and his team.

His chest tightened. She looked exhausted—shadows under her eyes, tension in her shoulders. But her spine was straight. Her jaw set.

He moved toward her. "Agent Dawson—"

"Don't give me that *Agent Dawson* bullshit, Wolf. I need to be in this briefing." Her voice was steady. Not asking permission—stating a fact. "I know this man better than any of you in this room. You need me."

She was right. Damn it, she was right.

Garrett looked at Grizzly, then Lynx. Both were watching the exchange carefully. Waiting for his call.

"Fine," he said. "But after the briefing, you go back to your room, and you stay there."

"Agreed." Claire moved to the conference table and set down her laptop. "Where's Dr. Montgomery?"

"On her way," Lynx said.

As Grizzly headed out to set up post at the main entrance, Vivi entered, tablet in hand, looking like she hadn't slept in days. "Agent Dawson." Vivi's voice was warm despite the circumstances. "I'm glad you're here. We can use your expertise."

Claire let go of a heavy sigh. "Will everyone stop addressing me as Agent Dawson? Just Claire, please."

Vivi smiled. Garrett pulled out a chair for Claire. "Everyone, take a seat," he said. "Let's review everything from the top. The message tells us he knows Claire is in Montana, but it doesn't specifically mention this compound or that he's already in the area. However,"—he circled the end of the conference table, unable to stand still—"we need to assume both. We are Code Red until I ascertain our suspect is not outside our doors."

They took positions around the table. Garrett remained standing—too wired to sit, too focused to relax. Claire pulled up files on her laptop, and Lynx helped connect them to the main screen.

"We estimate that I've been the Countdown Killer's target for approximately six months," she said. Her hands were steady as she navigated her files, but Garrett saw the tension in her shoulders. The way her jaw tightened when the stalker's messages appeared on screen. "Possibly longer."

She pulled up a timeline. Dates. Incidents. Photos. "Six months ago, I started feeling watched. I didn't have any evidence. Just... instinct." She glanced at Garrett. "You know the feeling. When you're being surveilled."

He did. Every operator knew that crawling sensation between your shoulder blades. He nodded, encouraging her to go on.

"Four months ago, flowers were delivered to my

apartment. No card. No sender information. I reported it to building security. They had no record of a delivery."

"He hand-delivered them?" Vivi said.

Claire absentmindedly tapped a finger on her laptop. "That's my guess. Three months ago, a note arrived. Slipped under my apartment door." She pulled up a photo with an evidence bag. Through the plastic, they could read the handwritten note:

You couldn't save Lily. Can you save yourself?

Garrett's hands curled into fists. Lily's name. *Her name.* This predator was using his sister's death to terrorize CJ.

Claire didn't notice his reaction. She was focused on her presentation, clinical and detached. "I wrote it off as a crank. Two months ago, the surveillance became overt. He sent me photos of me at work, at the grocery store. Getting coffee. He wanted me to know he was watching."

More photos appeared on the big screen. Claire in the parking garage. Claire at a crosswalk. "The photos escalated. Closer angles. More invasive. And then, the killings started. I didn't connect them at first—not until I realized the women resembled me and were all survivors. Recently, he sent a package to me with this." She pulled up another evidence photo.

The bracelet. Silver. Delicate. Identical to Lily's.

"My best friend Lily was murdered fifteen years ago. She was wearing a bracelet like this when she died. I always wanted a matching one so we'd be twins." Claire's voice was steady, but Garrett heard the emotion underneath. "This isn't an exact replica, but it's close enough to send a message."

Vivi nodded. "As I suspected, he's not just targeting you as a survivor of violence. He's targeting you specifically because of your connection to Lily Harper."

"It appears so." Claire pulled up the timeline again. "Three days ago, I received the first direct threat. A message on my work computer, sent through an encrypted account."

The text appeared on screen:

You're all alone, Claire. Your friend couldn't outrun him. Will you outrun me?

"Meaning Collin Brands, the killer who took Lily and tried to take you?" Garrett asked.

Claire swallowed hard. "That's what we're assuming." She cleared her throat, but the emotions she was holding back were still evident in her eyes. "That's when SAC Reeves pulled me from the case and sent me here." Claire's eyes, so full of sadness mixed with determination, slid to Garrett again. "And now, tonight, he found me."

Garrett started pacing again. When he caught this asshole...

He took a deep breath and focused on the screen, not Claire's eyes. "How did you first connect him to the other three murders?"

"The messages. I ran a search through ViCAP for any murders involving victims who'd received repeated text messages before their deaths. I found three cases. All women who'd survived previous violence. All received text messages, as well as handwritten ones and gifts, before they were killed." Claire pulled up the victim files. "I saw their resemblance to me and that's when I knew."

Lynx looked up from his laptop. "And your team has no leads?"

"There's been no forensics at the crime scenes. He's careful. Meticulous." Claire's frustration was evident. "That's why I agreed to come here. Reeves thought that if I was off the board, he might make a mistake. Get sloppy."

Garrett realized that Reeves' earlier call about having potentially caught the guy was wishful thinking. "Instead, he got insider information and followed you."

He moved to the screen and studied the timeline. Six months of escalation. Photos. Messages. Gifts. All building to tonight. "Do you have a personal phone with you?" he asked.

Claire frowned. "In my room."

"I did a surface scan earlier," Lynx said. "Including both phones. They're clean."

Garrett motioned for her to follow him. "Let's get them. Now. Your clothes, shoes, and luggage, too." He met Lynx's eyes. "This time, run a deep diagnostic."

"Copy that," Lynx said.

Claire didn't argue. They went to the room, grabbed her belongings, and returned. They spread the items out on the empty end of the table, and Lynx used a handheld scanner on each piece.

"You think there's something in my underwear?" she asked Garrett, her cheeks tingeing pink as Lynx ran his scanner over a bra.

"We can't take chances," Garrett said, trying to avoid looking at the sexy lace. His mind instantly brought of images of her in it.

A minute later, Lynx plugged both her business and personal phones into his laptop and started running diagnostics. Thirty seconds later, his face darkened. He tapped the personal phone. "Spyware. Military-grade."

Claire went pale. "What?"

"He's had access to everything on this phone for—" Lynx narrowed his eyes as he scanned his screen. "Three months at least. GPS. Texts. Emails. Photos. Everything."

"Oh my god." Claire sank into her chair. "My texts to my parents. I told them I was going away for work. I didn't say where, but—"

"But your Bureau emails did," Garrett finished. "Did you access work email from this phone?"

"Yes. I—I wasn't thinking. I was packing, I checked my email one last time before I left D.C." She looked at him, horror in her eyes. "He saw it. He saw the protective detail authorization."

"Which is how he found you." Garrett turned to Lynx. "Destroy it. Now."

Lynx nodded before exiting the room with the phone.

Claire looked like she might be sick. "This is my fault. I led him right here."

"You've been under a lot of stress." Vivi's voice was gentle. "And he would have found another way. Predators like this don't stop. They adapt."

"Doc is right." Garrett sat down across from Claire.

Made her look at him. "You couldn't have known. But now we do. Which means we lock everything down. No personal devices. No outgoing communications. Nothing he can trace."

"Agreed." Claire took a breath, steadied herself. "What else do you need from me?"

He leaned back. This was going to hurt. But it had to be asked. "I need to know who you suspect."

"What?"

"Someone installed that spyware. Someone with access to your phone. Your apartment. Your life." He kept his voice even. "Who has that kind of access? A boyfriend? Neighbor? A coworker?"

"I don't—" She shook her head. "There is no boyfriend, and no one from work has ever been to my apartment. I don't know my neighbors that well."

"Which means he either has keys or knows how to bypass your security." Garrett had Lynx pull up building schematics on the screen. "Your apartment building— who has master keys?" he asked.

"Building management. Maintenance staff."

Lynx returned and gave him a nod to assure him the phone and spyware had been destroyed. Too little, too late, but they had no option but to move forward.

"I need their names," Garrett said to Claire. "All of them."

Claire rattled off several. Lynx started running background checks immediately.

"What about at headquarters?" Garrett asked. "Who has access to your office?"

"Everyone in my unit. Support staff. IT department."

"I need their names, too."

"You need the entire FBI employee list?"

"I'll handle it," Vivi said, touching her tablet.

Garrett nodded. "Tell me about SAC Reeves," he said to Claire.

Her head snapped up. "What about him?"

"How long have you known him?"

"Five years. Since I joined the Bureau."

"How *well* do you know him?"

"He's my supervisor. My mentor." Her voice had an edge now. "What are you asking?"

"I'm asking if there's any reason to suspect him."

Her body went rigid. "Marcus Reeves has thirty years of service." She stood, her hands flat on the table as she leaned toward him. "He's one of the most decorated agents in the Bureau. He's been my advocate, my teacher, my friend."

"Which makes him the perfect person to have access to your location, your schedule, your vulnerabilities." Garrett kept his voice level. He flicked his gaze to Lynx. "I need to know if he has any financial problems or relationship issues. Anything that could make him vulnerable to compromise."

Claire's voice rose a notch. "You're accusing my *SAC* of being the Countdown Killer?"

"I'm accusing no one. I'm investigating everyone."

"These are my people, Wolf." Her voice shook with barely controlled anger. "People I trust with my life."

"And one of them might be trying to end it." He

stood, placed his own hands on the table, and met her eyes. "That spyware didn't install itself. Someone had physical access to your phone. Someone close to you."

"It could have been anyone—"

"No. It couldn't." Lynx pulled up the tech specs on the main screen. "This is military-grade surveillance software. It requires specialized knowledge to install. Hell, I almost didn't find it."

Garrett studied it for a long moment, then turned back to Claire. "Whoever installed this is law enforcement or intelligence. My guess is intelligence. Someone with training and access."

Claire stared at the data. He could see her mind working. Her profiler's brain was connecting dots she didn't want to connect. "You think it's someone at the Bureau," she said with no emotion now.

She was slowly coming on board. He hated forcing her to face facts, but it had to be done. "I think it's someone with access, knowledge, and opportunity. That fits a lot of people at the Bureau."

Her voice was so quiet, it was nearly a whisper. "Including Reeves."

"Including Reeves."

She turned away, arms crossed. He could see her shoulders shaking. Not with fear. With fury.

"We need everything on him," Garrett said to Vivi. "His work history. His associates. His communications with Claire. Travel logs. Everything."

Claire whirled on him. "You want me to investigate my own SAC."

"I want you to help me eliminate him as a suspect. If he's clean, the investigation proves it. If he's not—"

"He's clean," Claire snapped. "Marcus Reeves is a good man."

He nodded. "Then proving it should be easy."

"You don't understand. These people are my family. My team. They've had my back for five years. They've kept me alive."

Garrett couldn't keep the frustration out of his voice. "Until someone in the group began stalking you. Or at the very least, gave your stalker a way to follow you no matter where you go."

Claire flinched. "SAC Reeves is the one who sent me here. If he's the Countdown Killer, why would he do that? You're not being logical."

Vivi stood. "Wolf is right, Agent Dawson." At Claire's fiery look, she cleared her throat. "Claire. And you're right, too—it doesn't make sense that Marcus would send you here if he were the killer. But we have to consider all possibilities."

Claire looked at Vivi. Then at Garrett. Then down at her hands. Garrett watched the wheels in her head spinning. She was damn good at her job, but she was also too close to this. It was messing with her head.

"What do you need?" Her voice came out resigned.

He and Vivi exchanged a loaded look. They'd won this scrimmage, but not the war. Not yet.

Vivi sat again. "I'll do the background checks, but we need you to tell us everything you can about your team. Your support staff. Anyone with access to your case files or your location. Especially their personalities and any odd quirks or insight into their psychological strengths and weaknesses."

Claire nodded, sat back down, and after a moment, started talking.

Lynx took notes. Vivi ran searches in real-time. Garrett listened to the tone of Claire's voice, mentally noting when she talked about anyone who made the timbre change or made her tense. She probably didn't even realize she was doing it.

It took an hour. By the end, Claire looked exhausted, defeated.

But they had what they needed—a list of suspects. People to investigate. Leads to follow.

"One more thing," Garrett said. "I'm instituting a new protocol. I'm moving into your room. Twenty-four-seven protection."

Claire looked up. "Moving *in*?"

He nodded. "Until we neutralize the threat."

"Can't you guard me from the hallway like you've been doing? I can leave the door unlocked."

"No." He pulled up compound schematics. "Your room has a window and is part of the ventilation system that connects to the outside. If he breaches the perimeter, I need to be directly between him and you."

Her voice rose again. "You think he could breach the perimeter? How? You've got layers and layers of security."

"We do, and I trust it, but systems fail. We will not underestimate him."

"We can put you in a closed environment with no windows," Vivi said, "but it's still connected to the ventilation system, and it's rather...sparse."

Claire studied the schematics. "Fine," she said on a heavy sigh. She was an agent. She understood tactical reasoning. "But I need boundaries. At least a little personal space."

Garrett had expected no less. "Understood. I'll stay near the door. I won't follow you into the bathroom, but you'll have time limits on showers, and you can't lock the bathroom door. You won't even know I'm there."

She looked at him—six feet two inches of armed SEAL—and something that might have been amusement flickered in her eyes. "Right. I definitely won't notice you."

Was that almost a smile?

HE MOVED his gear into her room an hour later. Go-bag, weapons, tactical equipment, all ready. Then, he set up a position near the door—chair, sleeping bag on the floor.

"I'll be here," he said as much to himself as to her. "Between you and any threat."

Claire slumped onto her bed, arms wrapped around herself. "This is surreal."

"It's also necessary."

"I know." She looked at him. "I'm sorry I fought you about Reeves. About the team. I know you're doing your job."

"No apology necessary. None of us wants to consider that our friends, family, or coworkers could be monsters."

"Yeah. It hurts." She pulled her knees up to her chest. "These people are my family. The idea that one of them could be—"

"I hope you're right about them," he said. "I hope they're all clean. But I have to check. You understand that."

"I do." She was quiet for a moment. "For what it's worth, thank you. For taking this seriously. For protecting me."

"It's what I do."

"It's more than that." Her eyes met his. "You could have assigned this to Grizzly or Hawk. But you're here. Why?"

Because I promised your best friend I'd take care of you. Because I failed once, and I won't fail again. Because you're CJ, and I can't lose you, too.

"I'm the Commander. I lead by example, and your safety is on me," he said.

The weight of those words hung in the air.

Claire nodded slowly. "I feel safer with you than anyone else."

His chest squeezed. He gave a nod. "Good. That's exactly what I'm here for."

GARRETT CHECKED HIS WATCH. Two A.M. Neither of them was sleeping.

He sat in the chair, weapon in hand, blocking the

door and keeping an eye on the window. He'd checked the lock three times and made sure the curtains were drawn tight.

Claire lay in bed, staring at the ceiling. "Wolf?" Her voice was quiet in the darkness.

"Yeah?"

"About earlier. When I asked about your sister." She paused. "I'm sorry I pushed. That was out of line."

His stomach tightened. "Don't worry about it."

"For what it's worth, I understand that pain. Losing someone and wondering if you could have saved them. If you could have done something differently."

"Yeah. I know you do."

He felt her shift to look at him. "Do you ever stop wondering?" she asked.

"No, but you learn to live with it."

"How?"

"You save the next person. And the next one. And the one after that." His eyes met hers across the dim room. "Until maybe one day, the scales balance."

Claire tugged the blanket closer around herself. "Do they ever? Balance?"

"I'll let you know if I get there." He saw her nod. "I know it's hard to shut down your brain, but try to get some sleep. We have a long day tomorrow, and I need you sharp."

"What about you? When will you sleep?"

"I'll sleep when you're secure."

She sank back down, turning toward the wall. "Thank you."

The words settled into his chest. He leaned back in the chair and focused on her breathing as it smoothed out and grew deeper.

A few hours later, there was a knock on the door.

Garrett moved automatically, weapon out and positioning himself between the door and Claire. "Who is it?"

"Vivi," came the reply.

He popped open the door. The doctor had been up all night. Her hair was pulled back, exhaustion in her eyes, but something else too.

Fear.

"I need to show you both something," she said.

Claire was already out of bed and standing next to him. "What is it?"

Vivi entered. "I've been working on the Trident profile since we parted. Cross-referencing the Countdown Killer's behavior patterns with historical case data." She pulled up her analysis. "The way he targets survivors. The way he references their original trauma. The specific details he knows."

"And?" Garrett asked.

"He knows too much." Vivi's voice was tight. "Details about the victim's orginial attacks. Details about Lily Harper's murder that weren't in public case files."

Claire went pale. "I've been over those case files and didn't pick up anything like that."

"Not about Lily. About you." Vivi met Claire's eyes. "About what happened between you that night. Outside of the facts you shared with law enforcement and your family that were never reported to the public, things only you and the killer would know."

Garrett's blood went cold.

"My interviews were all sealed," Claire said. "None of it was made public."

Vivi only nodded, staring at Claire, as if she could will her to understand.

And then Claire did. "You're saying the Countdown Killer has access to sealed case files?" Claire asked. "*My* files."

"Or he was there," Garrett said. "He was a witness. That's how he knew about the bracelet."

Claire stumbled back several feet. "No, there was no one there. There were no witnesses besides me and Lily."

"And the killer, Collin Brands," Vivi added.

Claire was shaking. "But he's dead."

Vivi was quiet for a long moment. "I think the Countdown Killer didn't just study Lily's case." She glanced between them. "I think he knew Brands. He may have even worked with him, learned from him." She paused, focusing on Claire. "You were highly traumatized that night. You suffered from a concussion. He might have been there, Claire, and you just don't remember."

All the color drained from her face. "You're saying the Countdown Killer was there the night Lily died?"

"I'm saying he knows things only someone there could know." Vivi pulled up more data. "In one note, he mentions you slipped and fell. In another, that you lost your shoe when you ran." Her eyes met Claire's. "He was either there, or Brands shared those details with him before he died."

Claire's voice shook. "So the Countdown Killer has been watching me for fifteen years?"

Garrett forced himself to stay calm. "Why wait till now to target her, Doc?"

"Because something has triggered him. It might even be the fifteenth anniversary."

Claire pinched her eyes shut. "Of course. The anniversary of Lily's death is in three days." She opened her eyes and locked on to Garrett's. His stomach was a rolling ball of centipedes. He'd been marking off the days, but it hadn't clicked for him either until right now. "That's what all of this has been building up to, and I didn't even see it. What kind of agent am I?"

He couldn't stop himself. He reached out and squeezed her arm. "He's been playing a game with you. It's time for us to turn the tables on him."

She moved closer, staring up into his eyes. "How?"

He forced a grim smile. "Thought you'd never ask."

CHAPTER SIX

Claire sat across from Dr. Montgomery in what the Shadow Point team called the 'interview room.' It looked more like a therapist's office than an interrogation space—comfortable chairs, soft lighting, a box of tissues on the side table. A pair of bonded parakeets trilled every once in a while, lending a touch of beauty and lightness to the room.

But Claire knew that was exactly what this was—an interview. A psychological profile. An excavation of her worst memories.

Wolf stood behind the one-way mirror in the observation room. She couldn't see him, but she felt him there. Watching. Listening. Learning things about her she'd spent fifteen years trying to forget.

"Take your time," Vivi said gently. "I know this is difficult."

Claire wrapped her hands around the mug of tea someone had given her. "What do you need to know?"

"Everything. Start from the beginning. The night Lily died."

The night that divided Claire's life into before and after. The night that made her who she was. The night she'd relived a thousand times in therapy, in nightmares, in the quiet moments when her guard was down.

Detach from the trauma. Report the facts. "We went to see a movie," Claire began. "It was a Friday night in September. We were fourteen. Lily's mom had dropped us off at the theater at seven. We were supposed to call when it was over for a ride home."

"But you didn't."

"No. We decided to walk. It was only a mile. We'd done it before." Claire stared into her mug, seeing a different time and place. "It was warm that night. We were laughing and talking about the movie. About boys. About nothing important."

The doctor's pen scratched on her notepad. "What happened next?"

"A car pulled up beside us. A man asked for directions." Claire's hands tightened on the mug. "We stopped. We were stupid, naive fourteen-year-old girls who didn't think anything bad could happen to us."

"You weren't stupid," Vivi said quietly. "You were children."

Claire had heard that so many times it didn't mean anything anymore. "He got out of the car. I remember thinking he was too close. Something felt wrong. I grabbed Lily's arm, told her we should go."

"Did she listen?"

"She started to, but he moved so fast. He grabbed me. I hit him, screamed, fought." Claire's voice cracked. "He twisted my arm and hit me in the head with a rock. Everything went gray and fuzzy. I vomited."

"What's the last thing you remember?"

"Lily screaming my name. And me on the ground. I tried to get up. Tried to help her. But everything was spinning. I couldn't make my body work." Tears burned behind Claire's eyes. She blinked them away. "I heard the car drive away. Heard Lily still screaming. And then... nothing."

"You lost consciousness."

"When I woke up, I was in the hospital. My parents were there. The police." Her voice hitched. " And Lily was gone."

Vivi leaned forward. "According to the hospital report, your skull was fractured."

"I was in the hospital for a week."

"And your memory of the attack?"

"Fragmented." Claire finally looked up and met Vivi's eyes. "I gave the police a description of the man. White male, thirties or forties, dark hair, average height. But it was dark, and after he hit me, all I wanted to do was get away. They showed me photo lineups. Sketches. I couldn't identify him with certainty."

"That must have been frustrating."

"It was torture." Claire's voice was raw now. "They found Lily three days after I got out of the hospital in a field twenty miles from the abduction site. The medical examiner said she'd been alive for at least thirty-six hours after she was taken. Thirty-six hours that I could have saved her if I'd just remembered his face. If I'd been stronger. If I'd fought harder."

"You have to quit blaming yourself."

"I failed her." The truth that lived in her chest like a stone. "I was supposed to protect her. We were best friends. And I let him take her."

"Why do you think Brands didn't take you?"

She'd been over that thousands of times in her mind. "Because I fought back? Because he didn't want to deal with a damaged girl with a broken arm and a concussion?" She shrugged. "When they caught up to him, he committed suicide by cop, so they couldn't get answers."

"Tell me about Lily," Vivi said. "Not the night she died, but who she was."

Claire's throat tightened. "She was smart and sarcastic. She wanted to be a marine biologist. She loved the ocean. We'd planned this trip to California the summer after we graduated high school. We were going to drive up the coast, see the redwoods, and visit Monterey Bay."

"You loved her."

"She was my sister in every way that mattered." Claire's voice broke, and a tear slipped out of her eye. She hurriedly wiped it away. "I didn't have any siblings, and she had a brother, but he lived with their dad. I only met him once or twice when he came to visit."

Claire paused, trying to pull up the memory. It was hazy, distant. "I saw him at the funeral. He looked...destroyed. Like part of him had died with her. I wanted to say something to him. Tell him I tried to save her, but all I could get out was, 'I'm sorry.' I was broken, and I didn't know what to say to the brother of the girl I couldn't save."

The doctor's pen did more scratching.

Claire closed her eyes. "Lily talked about him sometimes. Said he was in trouble a lot as a kid, but was getting his life together. He called her every Sunday night. She wouldn't go anywhere, always waiting for that call, but that weekend he couldn't. He told her he was going out with friends. She'd been devastated and I'd suggested the movie." She blew out a deep breath, her lips vibrating from it. "If only he'd kept to the schedule, or I hadn't convinced her to go out..." If onlys had tormented her all these years. "But my memories of him are vague. Just... a tall kid at a funeral who looked like his world had ended."

She'd known exactly how he felt. Her own world felt the same way and—

Her vision tunneled. Her lungs froze. She tried to breathe. Couldn't. Her chest was too tight. The air too thin. The walls too close.

"Claire?" Vivi's voice came from far away. "Claire, look at me."

But she couldn't. She was back there. On the ground. Watching Lily being dragged away. Screaming her name. *Failing. Failing. Failing.*

Her vision narrowed even more, spots dancing at the edges, closing in. Her hands were numb. Her heart was racing so fast it hurt.

"I can't—" she gasped. It was a panic attack. She hadn't had one in years. The therapy had fixed this, taught her how to control her emotions. "I can't...breathe. I can't—"

The door burst open. Wolf dropped to his knees in front of her. "Claire. You're okay. Look at me."

She couldn't. The room was spinning. Lily was screaming. Bobby was at the funeral. The man in the car. The bracelet. The countdown. Three days until the anniversary. She'd failed. She'd failed. She'd—

"Claire." Wolf's voice was firm, grounding. "Eyes on me. Right now."

The command cut through her spinning thoughts. She forced herself to focus. His green eyes were so steady. Calm. Alive.

"Breathe with me," he said. "In for four. Hold for four. Out for four. Can you do that?"

She tried. Failed. Gasped.

"You can do this." His hands found hers, solid and warm. "In. Two. Three. Four. Hold." She did it. Not as smoothly as his voice coaxed her to, but as best as she could. He squeezed her hands in encouragement. "Two. Three. Four. Good. Now, out. Two. Three. Four."

Vivi's voice joined his, softer. "You're safe, Claire. You're in Montana. You're at Shadow Point. The man who took Lily is dead. You're safe."

"In. Two. Three. Four."

Claire's lungs found rhythm following Wolf's voice. His hands warmed hers, his eyes anchored her.

"That's it. Again." He breathed with her, exaggerating his inhale. "In. Two. Three. Four."

The room stopped spinning. The dots receded. Her heart slowed its frantic race.

Wolf was so steady. So calm. "Keep breathing. You're doing great."

Vivi stood. "I'm going to get you some coffee and sugar. Be right back."

The door closed. It was just Claire and Wolf, her hands still in his. His eyes continued holding hers.

"I'm sorry," Claire whispered. "I haven't had a panic attack in years. I thought I was past them."

"Trauma doesn't work like that." His voice was rough. "It waits. Hides. Sneaks up on you when you're not looking."

"It's snuck up on you, too, hasn't it?"

Something flickered in his eyes. "More times than I care to admit."

Claire realized she was still gripping his hands. She should let go. Should pull back. Should re-establish professional distance.

She didn't.

"Can you stand?" Wolf asked.

"I think so."

He helped her up, his hand on her elbow. Steady. Strong. Safe. "I can take you back to your room."

Claire's hands fisted in his shirt. She couldn't let go. Didn't want to let go. She needed him close. Needed his strength because hers was gone.

"Claire?"

"Please." Her voice broke. "Just... Stay with me right here for a minute. I need something to hold on to."

Wolf tensed, his discomfort radiating through him, but he didn't pull away. "I've got you. You're okay."

She believed it. Something deep inside her let go of the tension. "Thank you for understanding. For not...you know."

Slowly, carefully, his arms came around her. One hand on her back. One on her head, cradling her against his chest. "I do know. You're incredibly strong and brave, but it's okay to acknowledge you've been through a trauma."

Yes. It was nearly impossible for her to do, but she knew he was right. Her therapist had told her that same thing over and over again.

Until now, in this moment, she'd refused to go there. Refused to let herself show any weakness.

But in the safety of his arms, she knew he didn't see her as weak. He saw her for who she was—*strong and brave*, even if she'd been through hell.

She closed her eyes, and her breathing became easy. So easy. His heart beat steadily under her ear. His chest rose and fell in a rhythm her body matched. He smelled like soap, his tactical gear, and something else.

Safety.

"Tell me something," Wolf said quietly. "Something good. A favorite memory."

"What?"

"Anything. Your favorite food. A place you've traveled. Just...something that isn't this."

Claire chuckled. "Ice cream. Cookie dough ice cream

from this place in Georgetown. Lily and I would beg her mom to take us there every Saturday in the summer."

"What else?"

"Books. I read everything. Thrillers, mysteries, sci-fi. Anything that takes me out of my head for a while."

"Do you have a favorite?"

"The Martian. I've read it five times."

She felt rather than heard his almost-laugh. "Stranded on Mars. Sounds relaxing."

"It's about survival. Problem-solving. Not giving up even when everything's against you."

"No wonder you like it."

Claire pulled back slightly, just enough to look up at him. His face was inches from hers. This close, she could see those gold flecks in his green eyes again. The small scar above his left eyebrow. The way his lips quirked with what seemed like genuine pleasure that he'd made her forget the bad memories. That she was clutching him like a lifeline.

"This is your brand of therapy, isn't it?" she asked. "I like it."

"It's nothing."

"It's not nothing." She should step back. Should let him go. "You talked me out of a panic attack and got me back on an even keel."

"Yes, I did," he said a little cheekily.

She pinched his side. "Don't get arrogant, Commander."

The term seemed to remind him of where they were.

Who they were. He gently but firmly stepped back, disengaging her hands from his shirt.

"Sit," he said, easing her back into the chair. His voice was still light as he added, "Doctor's orders."

Her legs were still shaky, but she was steady now. Her heart rate was normal.

"Have you had therapy?" she asked.

Wolf's expression shuttered. "Some."

"Did it help?"

"I'm still here."

She smiled. "I'm glad."

He smiled back. "At the moment, I am, too."

Heat spread through her body. She tried to think of something to say, but her brain seemed to short-circuit.

He came to the rescue. "What about your family? Your parents. They must be proud of you. FBI agent, catching killers."

"They are." Claire wrapped her arms around herself, suddenly cold without his warmth. "But they moved to France five years ago. My dad's company transferred him to Paris. They wanted me to come with them, but I stayed."

"For the job."

"For Lily." The truth she'd never said out loud. It startled her in some ways, but in others, it seemed exactly right. "I couldn't leave. Couldn't stop hunting men like the one who took her. It felt like... if I left, if I gave up, she'd die all over again."

Wolf was quiet for a long moment. "She wouldn't want you to sacrifice your life for hers."

"No, she wouldn't, but that doesn't bring her back."

"You're too hard on yourself. No one who loves someone wants them to stop living because they're gone."

The weight in his voice. The certainty. Claire studied his face, this man who understood grief in a way most people didn't. "Are you insinuating I stopped living because of what happened?"

"Have you? Is everything you do for her?"

Her hands found a thread on her sleeve. "Now you do sound like a therapist."

He must have heard the annoyance in her tone. He raised his hands in surrender. "Sorry. I was out of line."

He was, and yet, she realized she was bristling because he'd hit the nail on the head. Who would she be right now if she hadn't been living for Lily?

Rubbing her forehead, she sagged back in the chair. She'd think about that later. "What about your family?" she asked. "Your parents. Do you see them?"

Wolf's jaw tightened. "No."

"Why not?"

"We don't have that kind of relationship."

"I'm sorry."

"Don't be." He faced the two-way mirror, his attention landing on her reflection. "Doctor Montgomery should be back soon with that coffee."

Deflecting. Again. Every time Claire got close to something real, he pulled back.

"Wolf—"

"Tell me how you track killers," he said, turning to face her. "Your process. step by step."

Claire sighed but accepted that he was a closed book. For now. She was a profiler, and soon, she'd figure him out. "I look at victimology—who they target, why—and apply pattern analysis. Then I look at geographic profiling—where they hunt. Behavioral markers—escalation patterns, cooling-off periods. I put it all together and build a psychological profile. It includes what drives them, what triggers them, and what they need."

"And once you have that?"

"It's more science than art, but once I have all of that, I'm more accurate at predicting their next move. If the team agrees, we set up surveillance on likely targets or locations and wait for them to make a mistake."

Wolf crossed his arms over his impressive chest and leaned back on the wall. "What if we don't wait?"

"What do you mean?"

"The Countdown Killer wants you. He's obsessed with you. What if we use that?"

Claire's pulse sped up. "You mean as bait?"

"I mean, we set a trap. Make him come to us on our terms."

"I've been thinking the same thing." Claire leaned forward. "What if I reach out to him? Post something online where he'd see it. Something that makes him think I want to meet. To end this. To finish what started fifteen years ago."

"No." Wolf's voice was steel.

"Why not? It makes tactical sense. He's looking for me anyway. This way we control—"

"No." He pushed off the wall. "You're not dangling yourself in front of a serial killer."

"I'm an FBI agent. I've done undercover work before."

"Not with someone who's obsessed with killing you specifically."

"That's exactly why it would work."

"That's exactly why it's too dangerous." His eyes were hard. "We'll set a trap, but not with you as bait."

"Then how?"

"We use the spyware against him. He had access to your phone. He thinks he knows you. Knows how you communicate. We use the phone to send messages he believes come from you."

"You pretend to be me."

A nod. "I respond to his next message. Tell him I'm tired of running. He's outsmarted me and the entire FBI. I want to meet face-to-face."

"He'll know it's not me."

"Will he? He's been watching you from a distance. Reading your texts. Your emails. Does he know how you think when you're cornered? Even if he's one of your coworkers, he can't predict how you'll react. Taking the doctor's theory into account, he's only ever seen you as a fourteen-year-old victim or a competent FBI profiler. I can pretend to be you."

"This is insane."

"This is tactical."

Vivi entered with a tray—three cups of coffee, sandwiches, and a concerned expression.

"How are you feeling?" she asked Claire.

"Better. Thank you."

She set down the tray, handed Claire a coffee loaded with cream and sugar. "Drink. You need the calories, and the sugar will help stabilize you."

Claire sipped. It was too sweet, but warm. Grounding. "Wolf was just explaining his plan to trap the Countdown Killer, using my phone to lure him in."

Vivi glanced at Wolf with a quirked brow. "How?"

Wolf shrugged. "If he sends another message, I respond as Claire. I can set up a meeting. Somewhere we control. Somewhere we can take him alive."

"You want to take him alive?" Claire asked.

Wolf snagged a cup of coffee and smiled. "Dead men can't tell us if they were at Lily's murder or if there are more victims we don't know about. You need closure. You need to bring him to justice."

Vivi considered this. "It has merit. The Countdown Killer is arrogant. He's been playing games with you for months. If you offer to meet on his terms, he might take the bait."

"I hate this plan," Claire said. "But it might work."

"We'd need the right trigger," Vivi said. "Something that would make Claire reaching out believable."

"The anniversary," Claire said quietly. "I could say I want to end it on the anniversary. Poetic justice. He'll eat that up."

Wolf's eyes were dark. "Exactly."

They sat in silence for a moment, drinking and eating while they all stewed over the plan.

A phone buzzed. All three of them froze.

"Is that yours?" Wolf asked her.

Claire pulled out her Bureau-issued phone. Looked at the screen.

Unknown Number.

Her hands shook as she unlocked it and read the text message.

The world fell silent, a roaring in her ears blocking it out.

Bobby couldn't save her either.

The phone slipped from Claire's fingers.

Wolf caught it. Read the message. His face went gray. Something terrible flickered behind his eyes.

"Why would he say that?" she asked. "Bobby wasn't even in town that weekend."

Wolf said nothing. Just stared at the message as if it had physically wounded him.

Vivi took the phone. Read it. Looked at Wolf with an expression Claire couldn't read.

"He knows about Lily's brother," Vivi said. "That's not a surprise, but it is interesting that our killer would mention him."

Claire bolted upright. "Oh god. What if he's gone after Bobby? What if—"

"I'm sure he's fine," Wolf said. "We need to stay focused on you."

Claire's mind raced, ignoring him. "I don't know where he is. I haven't seen him since the funeral. He'd be... what, thirty-three now? He could be anywhere."

"We'll look into it," Wolf said. "Don't worry about him."

"He could be in danger. Why else would the Countdown Killer mention him?" Claire asked.

Wolf's eyes met hers. They were shuttered, but she saw anger and something that reminded her of resolve behind them. "Because he wants you to think that no one can save you," he said. "Not the FBI. Not Shadow Point." His voice dropped. "Not Bobby."

The coffee turned sour in her stomach. "Well, he's wrong. First of all, I don't need saving, and secondly..." Her gaze stayed locked on Wolf. "I've got you."

CHAPTER SEVEN

Bobby couldn't save her either.

The words burned in Garrett's mind like acid. Fifteen years of carefully constructed distance between Bobby Anderson and himself evaporated with five words on a screen.

He stood in the command center, staring at Claire's phone, his hands shaking with a rage he hadn't felt since Colombia. Since the night he'd hunted down the man who'd been torturing local women. Since he'd crossed lines he could never uncross.

The Countdown Killer wasn't just taunting Claire.

He was taunting *him*.

"Commander?" Lynx's voice pulled him back. "You want me to trace this?"

Garrett forced his jaw to unclench. "Do it. Now."

His team moved. Lynx was at his laptop, fingers flying. Grizzly was checking perimeter alerts. Hawk was pulling up surveillance feeds. And Vivi watched Garrett with those too-knowing psychologist eyes.

Claire sat in the corner, still pale from the panic attack. Still shaken from the message. Looking at him like she was trying to solve a puzzle with missing pieces.

He couldn't meet her eyes. If he did, she might see the truth written all over his face.

Bobby couldn't save her.

Because Bobby had been eighteen and stupid and a hundred miles away when Lily was taken. Because Bobby had failed in every way that mattered. Because Bobby was weak.

But Garrett wasn't.

"Got it." Lynx looked up, his face grim. "Message originated from Blackridge."

The room went silent.

"Blackridge," Garrett repeated. His voice was hollow. "He's here."

"Could be using a relay," Hawk offered. "Spoofing his location."

"Or he's actually here," Grizzly said. "In town. Close enough to see the compound."

Garrett's blood ran cold. The stalker wasn't in D.C. anymore. He'd followed Claire to Montana. Maybe watching the compound and planning his next move.

"How close?" Garrett asked.

Lynx pulled up a map. A red dot blinked in the center of town. "Signal came from downtown. The coffee shop next to The Last Stand has public Wi-Fi. He could have sent it from inside or from a vehicle outside."

Claire rose, a ghost of herself, moving toward the blinking light.

"Surveillance footage?" Garrett barked.

"I'm pulling it now, but—" Lynx shook his head. "It's a busy coffee shop. A dozen people inside. Another dozen walking past. He could be any of them."

"Or none of them," Claire said quietly. "He could have used a remote device and sent the message without being physically present."

Garrett wanted to put his fist through a wall. Wanted to get in his truck and drive to Blackridge and tear the town apart until he found the bastard.

But that's what the killer wanted. To make him sloppy. Emotional. Reactive.

Garrett Cross didn't get emotional. He planned, stalked, just like his call sign. The serial killer was about to come up against a fellow predator.

"We need to reply," Garrett said.

Claire's gaze snapped to his. "What?"

"This is our chance." Garrett moved to the conference table and pulled up a map of the area. "He wants to play games. We play better. Time to set the trap."

"What do you want to say?" Lynx asked.

Garrett studied the map. Abandoned warehouses. Industrial areas. Places outside town where they could control the terrain. Where the stalker would feel like he had the advantage, but Shadow Point would own every angle. He even considered his own shabby cabin. Talk about poetic justice if he could lure this bastard to that and bring Lily the justice she deserved.

"Claire tells him she's tired of running. Wants to end this. Face to face. On the anniversary."

Claire nodded. "But you're going to be waiting."

Garrett pointed to a location on the map. "This old mining facility is ten miles outside Blackridge. It's been abandoned for twenty years."

Grizzly nodded. "I know the place. It has multiple entry points, good sight lines, and it's isolated. Perfect for an ambush."

"His ambush or ours?" Lynx asked.

"Ours." Garrett looked at his team. "He thinks he's hunting Claire. But we'll be hunting him."

"He's too smart for that," Claire said. "He won't just walk into an obvious trap."

"He will if we make it believable." Garrett turned to her. "You're exhausted. Broken. Desperate. The message needs to sound like you're at the end of your rope. Like you'd rather face him on your terms than spend another day waiting for him to strike."

"He won't believe I'd agree to meet him alone."

"You're going to tell him to bring one person— someone to witness. Make it sound like you want an audience. Like this is your grand finale." Garrett's voice was cold, calculated. "Predators like him want recognition. Want their genius acknowledged. We give him that."

Vivi frowned. "It's risky. If he suspects for even a moment—"

"Then we adjust. Right now, we have one advantage: he doesn't know we know he's in Blackridge. He thinks he's still hidden. Anonymous." Garrett looked at each of them. "We use that."

"What do I say?" Claire asked quietly.

Garrett met her eyes. Saw the fear there. The exhaustion. The determination underneath.

He gestured at Lynx, who handed him the phone. He brought up the message and began Claire's reply. "*You're clearly intelligent and have outwitted all of us. I'm tired of this game and want to meet face-to-face. Let's do it on the anniversary of Lily's death.*"

"You really think he'll just... agree to that?" Claire asked.

"No. He'll counter and negotiate. But it opens the door. Gets him talking."

"Gives me a chance to trace more communications," Lynx said.

Garrett's jaw tightened. "And it tells him that you're breaking. That he's winning."

"He'll insist I come alone," Claire said.

"And it will appear that you are. You'll tell him you're going to ditch your security guards and do this your way."

"You're not going to let me within ten feet of the place, though," she said. "Are you?"

"Not even close."

"I hate this plan." She scraped her hair back. "I want to be there when you take him down. He should be my arrest."

He took a breath, softened his voice. "You hate any plan that isn't within your control. We all do."

"That's not—" She stopped. Exhaled. "Fine. I admit

that's true, but if you were in my shoes, you'd feel the same way."

He hesitated. She was right. "Fair point, but in this case, I need you to stay as far away from him as possible. Once we have him, you can officially arrest him. Deal?"

She narrowed her eyes, didn't agree. "What do I say about Bobby? The message mentioned him. I should address it, shouldn't I? Get him to explain himself?"

Garrett's chest constricted. "No."

"Why not?"

"Because that's not pertinent to the goal. He wants to see you react. To know he hit a nerve, but you barely knew this Bobby kid." Garrett kept his voice level. "You ignore it and focus only on the meeting. The anniversary. Make him think you're conceding."

Claire studied him for a long moment. Like she was trying to read something in his expression. He kept his face carefully blank.

"Okay," she finally said. "Send it."

Garrett hit Send.

Then they waited. Minutes stretched into an hour as the team monitored feeds, ran scenarios, and prepared for every possible response.

No reply came.

"Maybe he's not checking his phone," Hawk suggested.

"He's checking," Vivi said. "He sent that message to get a reaction. He's watching to see what she does."

"Then why isn't he responding?" Claire asked.

"Because he's toying with you," Garrett said. "He

knows instant responses look desperate. He wants to string this along, and he's taking time to analyze the message. Decide if it's genuine."

"Or he knows it's a trap," Grizzly added.

"Either way, he'll respond. He's come too far to let this slip away from him. We just have to wait him out." Garrett stood. "Grizzly, I want you on perimeter patrol. Hawk, rotate with Bobcat on overwatch. Lynx, continue monitoring all communications. If he responds, I want to know immediately."

His team moved out. He was soon alone in the command center with Claire and Vivi.

"You should rest," Garrett said to Claire.

"I'm not tired."

"You didn't sleep last night and had a panic attack two hours ago. Your body needs—"

"My body is fine." She crossed her arms. "What I need is to be useful. Not locked in a room while everyone else works."

"You *are* being useful. You gave us everything we need to catch this guy. Now you let us execute."

"This is my case, and I'm the target. I can't *rest*."

Time for a dose of her own medicine. "If the situation were reversed, and I was the one being stalked, what would you advise me to do under the circumstances?"

Claire's eyes flashed. "Reverse psychology won't work on me."

Vivi smiled.

"Come on," Garrett pressed. "Answer the question, Agent Dawson."

Her hands went to her hips. "Are you purposely trying to rile me up?"

"Whether I am or not, you're proving to me that you're overly emotional."

"I am not."

They stared at each other. Stubborn alpha meeting immovable alpha.

Vivi cleared her throat. "I'll check on the profile updates. Let you two... discuss strategy."

She left, grinning.

Garrett turned back to Claire. "Your room. Now."

"You're not my commanding officer."

"I'm the tactical commander of this operation, which means when it comes to your safety, yes, I am."

"This is ridiculous—"

"This is keeping you alive, Paperclip."

"Don't you dare call me that."

Garrett stepped closer. Close enough to see the exhaustion in her eyes. The fear she was trying to hide. "Please, Claire. Just... let me do my job."

Something in his voice must have gotten through. She deflated. "Fine. But I'm not staying in that room alone all night while you plan without me."

"Bobcat will take watch."

"What?" Her head snapped up. "Where will you be?"

"Here. Planning every single detail of the operation with my team."

"Then I'm staying here with you."

"No—"

"I'm the one he's hunting. I'm the one who knows his patterns. I'm the one who—"

"—is too close to this," Garrett finished. "You can't be objective about a predator who's obsessed with killing you."

"And you can? You lost your sister to a killer, too. You're just as compromised on this as I am."

The words hit like a gut punch. She didn't know how right she was.

"That's different," he managed.

"How?"

"It just is." Garrett headed for the door. "Let's get you back to your room."

"Wolf—"

He kept walking.

Claire's room felt smaller with both of them in it. Garrett grabbed his go-bag and checked his gear. Weapons, tactical equipment, extra magazines. He hated not being with her, but he needed to be in the op center. He couldn't exactly hold meetings in here. Let Bobcat take watch while he coordinated the details of what they'd do, no matter what stunt the killer tried to pull.

Because he would. Garrett didn't need to be a profiler or a psychologist to know that.

"What's that?"

Garrett turned. Claire was looking at his open bag. At the photograph tucked into the inside pocket. It had half fallen out.

His chest tightened. He quickly shoved it back inside and zipped the bag. "Nothing."

"Looks like a photo." She moved closer. "Is it of you and your sister?"

He should have hidden it better. Should have left it somewhere she couldn't see. But he'd needed it close. Needed the reminder of why he was here. Why he couldn't fail.

The photo was old. Two kids at a park. Lily, age ten, grinning at the camera. And Bobby, age fourteen, his arm around her shoulders. The last photo their mother had taken of the two of them before Lily died.

"It's private," Garrett said, keeping his back to her.

"You carry her photo with you. Just like I carry Lily's." She caught his eye and shoved the framed photo at him. "These photos remind us of why we do what we do."

He couldn't speak and barely glanced at it. His throat felt tight. His chest, too.

Her gaze dropped to his bag as she brought her framed photo to her chest. "Can I see yours?"

"No." He grabbed the bag's strap. "It's... I don't share it."

Claire's expression softened. "I'm sorry. I didn't mean to intrude."

"It's fine." It wasn't fine. Nothing about this was fine.

"What was her name? You never told me."

Garrett's hands stilled on his bag. This was dangerous territory. One wrong word and she'd start connecting dots. Would start seeing patterns. Would realize—

"I should go," he said.

"Don't change the subject. Your sister. What was her name?"

"Claire—"

"Please." Her voice was soft now. Vulnerable. "I told you about Lily. About the worst night of my life. I just... I want to know about yours."

He couldn't tell her. Couldn't say Lily's name and watch recognition dawn in her eyes. Couldn't risk everything. "She was a good kid. That's all that matters."

"Wolf." Claire's voice was strange now. Uncertain. "What was her name?"

"I need to go." He grabbed his bag and opened the door.

"Wolf, wait—"

He was out the door before she could ask again. The new man, Bobcat, was waiting. "Sir," he said, coming to attention.

"Bobcat, this is Agent Dawson." He motioned at Claire. "Claire, this is your new bodyguard."

Bobcat started to walk inside. Claire put a hand on his chest to stop him. "No."

Garrett sighed. "Claire."

She tossed Lily's picture on the bed and walked out of the room. "I'm coming with you."

"You need to stay in your room."

"And I told you I'm not sitting on the sidelines." She walked past him, chin up, spine straight. "I'm part of this operation whether you like it or not."

"Claire—" he tried again.

"I need to check in with my team at the FBI. Call

Reeves. Update them. Then I'm sitting in on your planning session because I know this killer better than any of you, and you need me there."

He hated it, but she was right.

"Fine." Garrett turned to Bobcat. "You're with us."

The three of them headed to the operations room, with its tactical maps, communication equipment, and enough weapons to supply a small army. Grizzly and Lynx were already there, studying satellite images of the abandoned mining facility. Hawk was outside, keeping eyes on the perimeter. Garrett sent Bobcat to back him up.

Lynx moved to his laptop. "All security monitors are operational. There are three drones in the air, and I've got eyes on every approach to the compound."

"Good." Garrett turned to Claire. "Make your call, but do not mention the new message. Do not mention our plan. Standard check-in only."

"Is that an order, Commander?" Claire said dryly.

"Yes, it is, Paperclip."

Rolling her eyes, she pulled out her Bureau phone and dialed Reeves. She put it on speaker so they could all hear. It rang four times and went to voicemail.

"Marcus, it's Claire. Just checking in. Everything's fine here. Shadow Point is...thorough. Call me when you can. I want to hear how the task force is doing."

She hung up. Looked at Garrett. "He should have answered. He always answers."

"Could be in a briefing," Grizzly suggested.

"At nine PM?"

"Or he's got his phone off. Sleeping." Lynx shrugged. "Even SACs need rest."

Claire didn't look convinced, but she didn't argue.

Garrett moved to the tactical map. "Okay. Let's assume the stalker takes our bait. Agrees to meet at the mining facility on the anniversary. Here's how we—"

The door burst open.

Vivi's face was pale, and her hands were shaking.

Garrett's blood went cold. "What is it?"

"Local police just reported a homicide." Vivi's voice was tight. "A woman, mid-twenties. brunette hair, blue eyes. Her throat was slashed."

The room went silent.

"Where?" Garrett asked.

"Behind the coffee shop where the message was sent." Vivi's eyes met his. "She looks like Claire."

Claire made a sound—something between a gasp and a sob.

The Countdown Killer wasn't waiting for the anniversary. Wasn't playing their game. He was hunting. Right now. In their town.

And he'd just killed a woman who looked like Claire. "He's not just here," Garrett added. "He just replied to our message."

CHAPTER EIGHT

A woman was dead.

A woman who looked like her—brunette hair, blue eyes, same build and features. Her throat had been slashed, and she'd been left behind a coffee shop in Blackridge like a message. Like a promise.

You're next.

The walls of the operations room closed in. Claire's chest tightened. Her vision tunneled. *Not again.* Not another panic attack. She'd just had one a few hours ago. She was past this, wasn't she? She could handle—

"Claire." Wolf's voice cut through the spiral. "Look at me."

She couldn't. The room was spinning. That woman. *Dead because she looked like me.*

Dead because the Countdown Killer was here. Dead because—

Strong hands gripped her arms. "Claire. Eyes on me. Now."

She forced herself to focus. Wolf's face. His green eyes. Steady. Solid.

"Breathe," he said.

"I can't—" Her voice cracked. "She's dead. She's dead because of me." She gulped air. "Because he couldn't find me, so he killed her instead and—"

"Up." Wolf pulled her to her feet. "We're leaving."

"What? No, I need to—"

But he was already moving, one arm around her waist, half-supporting her weight. Lynx and Grizzly exchanged glances. Vivi started to follow.

"Stay," Wolf said to Vivi. "Coordinate with the local PD. I've got her."

"Commander—" Vivi started.

"I've got her."

Claire barely registered the hallway. The turns. The door opening. Then she was in a different room. Smaller than hers and starker. A bed, a desk, tactical gear stacked on a chair No personal items. No photos. Nothing that made it feel lived-in.

Was this Wolf's room?

He set her in the desk chair, crouched in front of her. "You're not having a panic attack."

"I think I am."

"No, you're angry. Furious. And you're trying to bury it under guilt and shame. That's why you can't breathe."

Claire shook her head. "I'm horrified. I'm—"

His voice was hard. "That woman died because a predator is hunting you. You're enraged. You want to tear something apart. But instead, you're trying to be professional and controlled. The good FBI agent who doesn't lose her composure."

"I need to stay calm."

"You need to stop lying to yourself." He stood, crossed his arms. "Get angry, Claire."

"That's not—"

"Get. Angry."

"Stop it."

"He killed a woman tonight. Slit her throat and left her body like garbage. And he did it because he couldn't get to *you*. Because we're keeping you safe and it's pissing him off." Wolf's voice was relentless. "So he murdered an innocent woman to send you a message. To make you feel exactly what you're feeling right now. Guilty. Responsible. Like it's your fault."

"It *is* my fault—"

"It's HIS fault. He's the killer. He's the monster. And you're letting him win by drowning in guilt instead of fighting back."

Claire's hands curled into fists. "I am fighting back."

"Are you? Because from where I'm standing, you're falling apart."

She sucked in a breath. Her nails bit into her palms. "I'm doing everything I can. I came here. I gave you everything. I'm following your protocols and your plans and—"

"And you're still blaming yourself." Wolf leaned against the desk. "For Lily. For the three women in D.C. For tonight's victim. How much blood are you going to let him put on *your* hands before you get angry enough to stop him?"

"Don't talk to me like that."

His eyes were intense, unyielding. "You're doing the same thing now that you did fifteen years ago. Taking responsibility for something a monster did. Making his crimes about your failures instead of his choices."

"I should have saved Lily! These other innocent women!" The words tore out of her throat. "I should have been stronger. Faster. Better. I should have—"

"This is not your fault."

She was on her feet now, chest heaving. "I should have figured out the Countdown Killer before he killed three women. I should have caught him. I should have stopped him before he followed me here. Before he killed that woman tonight. I should have—"

"What? Been perfect?" Wolf's voice was quieter now. "Never made a mistake? Solved every case before anyone died? That's not how this works, Claire. You're human. You can't save everyone."

"Then what's the point?" Her voice broke. Something inside her broke along with it. Just...snap. "What's the point of any of this if I can't stop him? If people keep dying because I'm not good enough at my job?"

"Stop." Wolf's hands found her shoulders. "You *are* good enough. You're one of the best agents the Bureau has. You've caught seven serial killers and saved God knows how many lives. But you can't save everyone. No one can."

Tears burned behind Claire's eyes. She blinked them back. "That woman—"

"Is dead because the Countdown Killer murdered her. Not because you failed. Because he's a predator and that's what predators do." Wolf's grip tightened on her. "Get angry. Because anger is what's going to help you catch him. Not guilt. Not shame. *Rage.*"

Claire's breath was coming faster now. But not from panic. From fury. Building in her chest like a wildfire. "He killed her to hurt me," she said.

"Yes."

"He killed three other women because I wasn't fast enough."

"No, he killed them because he wanted to. Because he's evil. You didn't wield the knife. He did."

"But—"

"No buts. He's the killer. *But you're the hunter.* And right now, you need to decide which one you're going to be—the victim drowning in guilt, or the agent who takes him down."

Claire's hands were shaking from a rage so intense it felt like it might consume her. "I want to kill him," she whispered.

"I know."

"I want to make him suffer. Make him pay for every life he's taken."

"Good." Something fierce flickered in Wolf's eyes. "Use that. Channel it. Let it fuel you instead of destroying you."

Claire took a shuddering breath. Then another. The tightness in her chest was still there, but different now. Not panic. *Power.*

"That's it," Wolf said. "There's the agent I need. Not the one who falls apart. The one who fights back."

Claire looked up at him. This man, who barely knew her but somehow understood exactly what she needed. Who pushed her when she needed pushing. Who didn't let her drown in guilt. "Thank you," she said.

"Don't thank me yet. We still have to catch him."

"We will." The words came out with certainty she hadn't felt since this whole thing started. "We're going to find him. And we're going to end this." She shook a fist at the air. "*I will end this.*"

Wolf's mouth curved. Just slightly. "Careful. Keep talking like that, and I'll have to change your call sign to Fury."

The words hit like a match to gasoline. "Are you seriously joking about that right now?"

His bemused expression didn't falter.

Claire shook her fist again, this time directed at him. "You're joking about my call sign when there's a woman dead in Blackridge and—"

"There it is." Wolf's almost-smile widened. "That's the fire I need to see."

"You're unbelievable." She shoved his chest. Hard. "You push me to get angry, then you mock me—"

"I'm not mocking. Fury suits you better than Paperclip."

"I'll show you fury." She shoved him again. "You arrogant, manipulative—"

He caught her wrists. "Say it. You're furious with me right now. Admit it."

"Of course I'm furious with you!" She tried to pull away. Failed. "You're standing here smirking while—"

"While you're finally feeling something other than guilt." His voice was rough now. Intense. "While you're alive and fighting instead of breaking. While you're being the woman who's going to help me catch this bastard."

They were too close, his hands still around her wrists, gentle but firm. His eyes locked on hers. The air between them was charged with something that had nothing to do with anger and everything to do with the tension that had been building since the moment they met.

"Wolf?" Her voice was barely a whisper.

"Yeah?"

"I—"

She didn't finish. Couldn't. Because her mouth was on his, and every thought in her head evaporated.

He froze momentarily, then it was as if a switch had been flipped.

His hands released her wrists, slid to her waist, and pulled her closer. Her fingers fisted in his shirt, holding on like he was the only solid thing in a world that wouldn't stop spinning. The kiss was hard and desperate and real.

He tasted like coffee and something darker. Something dangerous. His stubble scraped her skin. His body was solid against hers—muscle and heat and barely controlled strength.

Claire pressed closer, needing more. Needing this. Needing him.

His hand slid into her hair, tilting her head back. The kiss deepened. Hungrier. More urgent. She met it eagerly, as if her grief and rage and loneliness had finally found an outlet.

His other hand moved to the small of her back, fingers splaying possessively. She gasped against his mouth. He took advantage, his tongue sweeping in, claiming her.

This was insane. Unprofessional. Reckless.

Claire didn't care. She kissed him back with everything she had. All the fear. All the fury. All the need she'd been suppressing since the moment she met him.

Wolf made a sound low in his throat. He backed her toward the desk, his hips pinning hers. She could feel every hard line of him. Could feel exactly how much he wanted this.

Her hands slid under his shirt. Warm skin. Raised scars. The body of a man who'd been to war and survived.

"Claire," he murmured, her name rough.

"Don't stop," she breathed.

"I should—"

"Don't."

His mouth moved to her jaw, her throat. She arched against him, head falling back.

A knock came from the door. They froze.

"Commander?" Vivi's voice rang out. "Is Claire okay? I wanted to check on her."

Reality crashed back in, cold and brutal.

Claire and Wolf stared at each other, his hands still on her. Her fingers were still under his shirt. Both of them were breathing hard.

"Oh my god," Claire whispered. "What are we—"

Wolf stepped back, releasing her and pulling away from her grip. He ran a hand through his hair.

Claire tried to straighten her clothes. Her hair. "We just—"

"Yeah."

"Wolf?" Vivi knocked again.

"She's fine," he called. His voice was steady and normal, like he hadn't just been kissing Claire as if his life depended on it. "Give us a minute."

There was a pause. "Of course. I'll be in the ops room."

Her footsteps retreated.

Claire stared at Wolf. This man, who'd pushed her to fury. Who'd just kissed her like—

"I don't even know your name," she said.

He went very still.

"Your real name. Not your call sign. Not Wolf." Claire's voice shook. "I just kissed a man whose name I don't even know."

Something flickered in his eyes. Something that looked like pain. He didn't say anything, though.

"What? Is it top secret?" She needed to know. Needed something real. "Please. Just tell me."

He opened his mouth. Closed it. The walls went up again, distance slamming back into place.

"We should get back to the team," he said. "We have a lot to coordinate with the locals."

"That's not an answer."

"It's the only one I can give right now."

Claire's chest tightened. She'd been vulnerable with him, and he wouldn't even tell her his name.

"Right," she said, straightening her shirt. "Dr. Montgomery is waiting." Claire couldn't look at him. Couldn't process what just happened. What it meant. What it didn't mean.

She opened the door. Vivi stood ten feet down the hallway, tablet in hand, expression carefully neutral.

Heat flooded Claire's face. Her lips were probably swollen. Her hair mussed. Her shirt wrinkled.

"Everything okay?" Vivi's voice was as neutral as her expression. "Was it another panic attack?"

Claire couldn't meet her eyes. "I'm fine now."

"Good. The team is reconvening in ten minutes. We have updates from local law enforcement."

"Of course. I'll—I'll be there."

Claire hurried past Vivi, head down, cheeks burning. She could feel the doctor's gaze following her. Analyzing. Understanding precisely what had happened in Wolf's room.

Behind her, she heard Wolf close his bedroom door.

"Commander." Vivi's voice was amused. "Interesting approach to panic management."

"Don't." Wolf's voice was tight.

Claire didn't wait to hear more. She fled down the hallway to the ops center.

Her lips still tingled. Her body still hummed with the memory of his hands. His mouth. The way he'd kissed her like she was everything.

And I still don't know his name.

Somehow, that felt like the biggest sellout of all.

CHAPTER NINE

Garrett watched Claire flee down the corridor, his heart still pounding, his lips still burning from the kiss.

What the hell had he just done?

He'd kissed her. Not just kissed—claimed her. Like she was his. Like he had any right to touch her when he was lying to her about everything that mattered.

I don't even know your name.

Her words cut deeper than the killer's knife. She'd trusted him with her body, her vulnerability, her rage. And he couldn't even give her his real name. Couldn't tell her he was Bobby. The boy hadn't been there for her or her best friend fifteen years ago.

That call...if only he'd kept to his schedule with Lily like Claire had said. None of this would have ever happened.

My fault, my fault, my fault.

He ran his hands through his hair, tried to steady his

breathing. This was exactly why he shouldn't have gotten close to her. Why he should have stayed professional.

But then she'd kissed him. Fifteen years of guilt and loneliness and need had exploded between them like a bomb. Yes, dammit, he knew that everything he'd said to her applied to him, too. In many ways, it wasn't his fault that Lily was dead—it was Brands who'd done it—but it didn't stop the clawing pain and guilt he'd always felt. One stupid phone call could have saved his sister.

Not only her, but all of the women the Countdown Killer had murdered, too.

He absentmindedly checked his tactical vest and his weapon. *Focus on the mission. Be the commander of this team.*

That's who he was now. Not Bobby. Not the failure. He was Wolf, commander of Shadow Point Security. He didn't let emotions compromise operations.

Vivi sidled up to him, her expression carefully neutral, but her eyes assessing.

"Don't," Garrett said.

"I haven't said anything yet."

"You're about to."

Vivi crossed her arms. "You need to tell her."

"No."

"Garrett—"

"My call sign is Wolf. That's all she needs to know."

"That's not what I'm talking about." Vivi shifted closer, lowering her voice. "It's clear she has feelings for you, and you for her. She trusts you, and you're lying to her about who you really are."

"I'm protecting the mission."

"You're protecting yourself." Vivi's tone was unrelenting. "And I understand why. But she deserves to know that you're Bobby. That you're Lily's brother. Especially if you've just crossed any unprofessional lines with her, which"—she glanced toward the ops room door closing behind Claire—"it looks like you have."

Garrett's jaw tightened. "Emotions are running high. I was only trying to help her, and..." He shook his head. "If I reveal who I am now, everything changes. She'll question why I didn't tell her immediately. She'll wonder if I've been using her. If this whole thing is about my guilt over Lily instead of keeping her safe."

"Isn't it both?"

Bam, bam, bam. Three words that landed like punches. The doctor was right. It *was* both. It had always been both.

"I'll tell her," Garrett said quietly, "after we catch this wackjob. After she's safe. When she can process it without the threat hanging over her head."

"That's not fair to her."

"Fair?" Garrett grunted. "For the first time since she arrived, she's not drowning in guilt over Lily. She's angry. Focused. Ready to fight. If I tell her now that I'm Bobby, that I've been skirting the truth this entire time, it will destroy that. She needs to hang onto her anger—not at me, at that bastard who's screwed up her life and is coming back for more."

"Or it will make her feel manipulated and betrayed when she finds out later." Vivi's expression was sympathetic but firm. "And she will find out. The longer you wait, the worse it will be."

"I know the risks."

"Do you? Because from where I'm standing, it appears you just kissed a woman who doesn't know your real identity. Who doesn't know you're connected to the worst trauma of her life. She believes you're her protector, not the brother of her dead best friend." Vivi paused. "That's not just dangerous for the mission. It's dangerous for both of you."

Garrett turned away and stared at the wall. Every word Vivi said was true. He knew it. Had known it from the moment he'd accepted this assignment and laid out his conditions.

But he couldn't tell Claire. Not yet. Not when they were so close to catching the predator who'd been hunting her. Not when she'd finally found her strength again. "I'll tell her as soon as we have the Countdown Killer in custody," Garrett said. "The moment he's neutralized, I'll sit her down and tell her everything."

"And if she hates you for deceiving her?"

"Then she hates me." Garrett didn't back down from Vivi's challenging gaze. "But she'll be alive. And the killer will be behind bars. That's what matters."

Vivi studied him for a long moment, then sighed. "You're walking a dangerous line, Commander."

"Been doing it my whole career, Doc."

"When this blows up, don't say I didn't warn you."

His chest felt like it was packed with concrete blocks. "I always give credit where it's due."

Vivi shook her head. "For what it's worth, even though I think you're making a mistake, I understand why you're making it. She's an incredible woman, and she looks at you like you walk on water."

Garrett didn't answer. What could he say? That he'd lost control of the mission the moment Claire had looked him in the eye? That fifteen years of wanting to protect CJ had finally broken through every wall he'd built? That kissing her had felt like coming home and losing everything all at once?

"Come on," Vivi said. "The team's waiting. And we have a killer to catch."

The ops room was tense when Garrett entered. Claire sat at the conference table, her posture rigid, her eyes carefully avoiding his. Lynx was at his laptop station. Grizzly stood near the tactical maps. Hawk had come in from perimeter patrol, leaving Bobcat on duty.

Everyone knew something had happened between him and Claire. The air was thick with unspoken questions. Garrett moved to the head of the table, all business. "What have you confirmed about the victim?" he asked Vivi.

"Her name was Rebecca Martinez. She was twenty-six, a dental hygienist, and lived three blocks from the coffee shop. No known connection to Claire or the other victims, but she got away from a serial rapist when she was seventeen and he was caught and imprisoned due to her testimony."

"Has the cause of death been determined?"

"The medical examiner has confirmed that the neck

wound was the cause of death. It was a single cut, left to right, and the same signature as the D.C. murders."

Claire flinched. Garrett saw it but didn't acknowledge it. Couldn't acknowledge it without everyone seeing too much.

"Time of death?" he asked.

Vivi peered through her readers. "Estimated between eight and nine. About an hour after we sent the message to the killer."

"So he killed her, then responded to our message by posting about it," Hawk said, a dangerous edge to his voice. "Sick bastard."

Claire's hands were clenched on the table. "He wanted me to know. Wanted me to feel responsible."

"Which is exactly what we're not going to let happen," Garrett said. The concrete in his chest still weighed him down, but he knew he had to keep Claire angry, not feeling guilty. "He's playing psychological games to disempower you. Are you going to let him do that, Agent Dawson?"

Her eyes met his. "Hell, no."

Garrett smiled. "Hell, no."

Claire's Bureau phone buzzed. She looked at the screen, her expression shifting. "It's Reeves."

"Answer it," Garrett said. "Put it on speaker."

Claire hit the button. "Marcus?"

"Claire." Reeves's voice filled the room. He sounded tired, stressed. "I'm sorry I missed your call earlier. I've been running down a lead."

"What kind of lead?"

"Your ex-boyfriend. James Cohen."

The room went still. Garrett watched Claire's face carefully. In it, he saw confusion, then recognition.

"James?" she shook her head. "I haven't talked to him in three years. We both had extremely stressful jobs and eventually realized it just wasn't working. We broke up and moved on. There's no way—"

"I know. I investigated him anyway so that we could rule him out." Papers rustled in the background. "James Cohen, thirty-two years old. D.C. lawyer working for the CIA's Office of General Counsel. Married eighteen months ago, has one kid. He's been thoroughly vetted by the Agency. Multiple background checks, polygraphs, the works. His wife confirmed he's been home every night for the past six months. Security footage from his office building corroborates his whereabouts during all the D.C. murders."

"So he's clear," Garrett said.

"Completely. No connection to the Countdown Killer. No motive or opportunity." Reeves paused. "But I did find something else while I was digging."

Claire leaned forward. "What?"

"I went to Derek, one of your IT support guys, to help me get the info on James. You know Derek?"

Claire's brow furrowed. "Derek Sullivan? Of course. He's been with the Bureau for... I don't know, as long as I have? He's always been really helpful whenever I have tech issues."

Garrett's instincts prickled. "What about him?"

"He hasn't shown up for work in two days," Reeves

said. "No call, either, to ask for time off. He has a spot-less record and has never even taken a sick day until now. His supervisor tried reaching him yesterday but there was no answer. Went by his apartment this morning. No one was home. His car's gone. It's like he vanished."

The room went silent.

"Two days," Lynx said quietly. "That's when Claire arrived in Montana."

"Could be a coincidence," Hawk offered, but his tone said he didn't believe it.

"Or it could be our guy," Garrett said.

Claire was staring at the phone as if it might explode. "Derek Sullivan." Her voice was incredulous. "You think Derek is the Countdown Killer?"

"I think the timing is suspicious," Reeves said. "I'm having his apartment searched right now, and we're checking all flights to Montana. So far, we've found nothing on the manifests under Derek Sullivan, but we're looking for anagrams and scrambled versions of his name in case he's using an alias. His computer forensics are being pulled. Financial records, travel history, everything."

"What's his background?" Garrett asked. "Military? Law enforcement?"

More page shuffling. "Former Navy. He was an electronics technician with four years of active duty and an honorable discharge. He joined the FBI as a contractor about five years ago, as Claire mentioned. He has a spotless record. No red flags." Reeves paused. "Until now. I'm sending you what we've got so far, Claire. Look it over and see what you think."

Claire's face had gone pale. "Derek was always so nice. So helpful. Whenever my computer crashed or my phone acted up, he'd fix it for me. He'd even come to my desk to help me in person if I couldn't figure something out."

Garrett's blood ran cold. "In person? He had physical access to your work computer?"

"And my phone," Claire said slowly. Her eyes widened. "Oh my god. He had my phone. Multiple times. He could have installed the spyware himself."

"How long have you known him?" Vivi asked gently.

"Since I joined BAU." Claire's voice was shaking. "He was just...Derek. Quiet. Friendly. Always willing to help. I trusted him."

"You know that's what predators do," Garrett said. "They build trust. Make themselves indispensable. Get close to their victims without raising suspicion."

Claire dropped her head into her hands and groaned. "It never crossed my mind that he was anything but a decent guy."

Lynx looked up from his screen. "Commander, Derek Sullivan legally changed his name before entering the Navy."

Everyone turned to Lynx.

"Changed it from what?" Garrett asked.

Lynx's face was grim. "Derek Brands."

The name hung in the air like a bomb.

Claire's mouth fell open. " As in...Collin Brands?"

Garrett felt like he'd been punched in the chest. "What's the connection?" Garrett forced the words out. His voice sounded distant, hollow.

Lynx was typing rapidly. "He's a distant cousin of Collin. Looks like they share a great-grandmother. Different branches of the family tree. No close contact on record, but..."

When he didn't finish, Garrett barked, "But what?"

"Derek's parents died when he was sixteen in a car accident. He went to live with relatives, including, briefly, with Collin's family." Lynx looked up. "He was seventeen when Lily Harper was murdered, and was living two hundred miles away with another branch of the family by then."

On the other end of the line, Reeves swore. "None of that surfaced in our investigation, but we just got started. Can you send me a copy of that for my team?"

Lynx glanced at Garrett. Claire did, too. "Of course we will," she said without waiting for his consent. "We're all on the same team here."

"I'll alert the local FBI office and get you whatever resources you need," the SAC said, then disconnected.

"So Derek knew Collin," Claire said. Her voice was shaking. "He knew the man who killed Lily. Maybe even..."

She couldn't finish. Didn't need to.

"Maybe he was there when it happened," Garrett said. The words tasted like acid. "The night Lily died. You said your memories were fragmented. That you couldn't remember clearly because of the head injury."

"I remember one man," she insisted. "But yes, I was concussed. Terrified. It was dark." Her hands were trembling. "There could have been two. Derek could have been there, and I just...I don't remember."

Vivi typed on her tablet. "That would explain how our killer knows details that were sealed in the case files about you."

Garrett's chest constricted. Derek had been there, or had at least known Collin Brands personally. If Collin had talked to him about his plans, Derek would have heard about Lily's family. About her half-brother, who rarely visited.

Would have known Bobby existed.

"Find him," Garrett said to Lynx. His voice was steel. "I want this bastard. Now."

"Already on it." The center screen filled with data Lynx was pulling. "But Commander, if he's as good as the spyware suggests, he'll be covering his tracks."

"Then we track him by what he can't hide." Garrett moved to the tactical map. "Blackridge isn't that big. He can't hide for long. The locals will flag him as an out-of-towner. We can use that to our advantage. We need boots on the ground in town, going place to place, home to home."

Garrett looked at his team. At Claire, still pale but determined. At Vivi, already lining up more operatives to join them. "This isn't only about stopping the Countdown Killer from targeting Claire."

"What do you mean?" Hawk asked.

Garrett's eyes met Claire's across the table. Saw the

same rage, the same need for justice burning in her gaze. "It's about finishing what started fifteen years ago," he said. "And making sure this predator never hurts anyone again."

On the main screen, a photo appeared. Derek Sullivan's FBI contractor ID. Brown hair, average features, unremarkable. The kind of face you'd see and forget.

Except Claire would never forget it now. And neither would Garrett. "Send it to our local law enforcement office," Garrett said. "I want everyone hunting him."

CHAPTER TEN

Derek Sullivan.

No. Derek *Brands*.

The name echoed in Claire's head like a curse. The helpful IT guy who'd fixed her computer a dozen times. Who'd come to her desk with a smile and patient explanations when her phone acted up. Who'd had physical access to her devices, been able to watch her at work, for five years.

He was Collin Brands' cousin. Had known the man who killed Lily. Had maybe even been there that night.

And she'd trusted him. The thought made her shudder. He'd been playing a long game all these years. Watching. Waiting. A spider who'd toyed with her, making sure she was secure in his web before he ate her.

Claire sat in the ops room, staring at Derek's FBI contractor photo on the main screen. The kind face that had made her feel safe asking stupid tech questions.

The face of a monster.

"Agent Dawson?" A voice pulled her back. One of the local officers was on speakerphone. "We need you to come down to the station as soon as possible. We have questions about Derek Sullivan's possible connection to our murder victim."

Claire blinked, forced herself to focus. "Of course. When?"

"Now would be best. We've put out an APB for him, based on what Shadow Point Security and the FBI have forwarded to us, but since you've flagged him as the Countdown Killer from D.C. and you're at the heart of the case, we need a statement directly from you."

"She'll do a phone interview for now," Garrett cut in. His voice was firm. "In-person tomorrow when the FBI team arrives from Missoula."

Silence on the other end. "And who are you?"

Vivi spoke up. "He commands my team, Officer Kent, and is currently Agent Dawson's bodyguard. I agree with his assessment—the best approach is for all three groups to meet tomorrow and share our collective intel at that time so we're all on the same page."

Kent wasn't pleased. "Dr. Montgomery, we have a murder victim and a suspect who's vanished. We need—"

"And you'll get my full cooperation," Claire interrupted. "But I've been targeted by this predator for six months. I'm exhausted, and I need rest before I sit in an interview room for hours."

Wolf's eyes met hers across the table. "A phone interview covers the immediate questions," he added. "You'll get a full debrief tomorrow when everyone's present, and we can coordinate properly."

More silence. A radio squawk sounded in the background. Ringing phones joined in. Several people were talking and calling out to each other. The small town police department had probably never had a murder. They were overwhelmed.

Kent gave a tight sigh. "Fine. But I want that interview within the hour. Detective Mills will call back at eight."

"I'll be ready," Claire said and disconnected. She'd wanted to argue. Wanted to say she could handle an interview right now, that she didn't need rest, that she was fine. But she wasn't. Her hands were shaking. Her chest felt tight again. Every time she blinked, she saw Derek's face. Smiling. Helpful. *Lying.*

She met Wolf's eyes. *Focus on the anger*, his stare reminded her.

"Lynx, set up a secure line for the interview," the commander said. "Doc, I want you present to monitor Claire's responses and cut it short if the locals push too hard."

"Copy that," Lynx said.

"I'll be fine," Claire insisted. If only she believed it.

Vivi moved to sit beside her. "You've been through multiple traumas in the past few days. A panic attack. A murder. Now finding out someone you trusted is connected to your best friend's killer." Her voice was gentle. "It's okay to not be fine."

"I need to be functional."

"You are, but you're also human." Vivi squeezed her shoulder. "Let us help you."

Claire's throat tightened. She nodded, not trusting her voice.

Wolf insisted she eat and took her to the cafeteria. There, he fixed sandwiches, grabbed chips, and poured them both energy drinks. He asked her about her experiences at the Bureau—not about Derek. The questions were thoughtful. His green eyes sparked when he teased her about being a badass.

She found herself relaxing for the first time in days. Weeks. Laughing and joking. Before she knew it, she'd finished off her entire meal.

He escorted her to her room and stood guard while she showered. She didn't spend too long in the hot water, but even the brief respite eased her tight shoulders. Her mind kept circling back to their earlier kiss. The fact that he was on the other side of the door made her body heat.

He was a good man, and she'd let herself get carried away with her emotions. But it had been too long since she'd felt safe. Desired. Too long since she'd allowed herself to feel more than passing friendship or affection for anyone.

She didn't need to be a profiler to realize it was because she'd been too scared of losing someone she cared about.

BACK IN THE OPS CENTER, the phone interview took forty-five minutes. The local detective was professional but relentless. How long had she known Derek Sullivan? How often did he have access to her devices? Did she ever suspect anything? Had he ever made her uncomfortable?

No. That was the answer that hurt most. No, she'd never suspected. He'd been invisible. Forgettable. Exactly what a predator wanted to be.

"Thank you, Agent Dawson," Detective Mills finally said. "The FBI team from Missoula will be here by ten tomorrow. We'll convene here at the station then for a full briefing."

"Understood."

The line went dead.

Claire slumped in her chair, exhausted. The adrenaline that had kept her going all day was gone, leaving her hollowed out and shaking.

"You did well," Vivi said quietly.

"I know what they're thinking." Claire's voice was flat. "I profile serial killers. Read people. See patterns. And I worked with him for five years and never once thought—"

"He was hunting you specifically," Garrett said. He stood near the tactical map, arms crossed. "He built a cover over the years. Got a job at the FBI. Positioned himself to have access to you without raising red flags. That's not something you could have anticipated or predicted."

"I should have."

"No." Garrett's voice was sharp. "You couldn't have known. Stop blaming yourself for what he did."

The words echoed what he'd said in his room hours ago when he'd pushed her to get angry instead of guilty.

"He's right," Vivi said with a patient smile. "Hindsight is twenty-twenty. Give yourself some grace."

Garrett sat across from her and kicked back, his gaze intense. "You're letting him get in your head again, Paperclip. That won't help anyone."

Claire glared at him. The man who'd helped her out of a panic attack. Who'd kissed her like she was oxygen. Who still wouldn't tell her his real name.

Something about him felt...familiar. Something in his eyes. The way he looked at her sometimes, like he was seeing more than just Agent Dawson.

"Get some rest," Garrett said. "Both of you. Bobcat will be at your door for a few hours before I relieve him, Claire. Grizzly is on perimeter patrol. Hawk's on overwatch. Lynx is monitoring systems. We're secure."

Vivi stood, grabbing her tablet and fighting a yawn. "And I've called in two other men with solid backgrounds to add an extra layer of eyes to our security setup overnight. Everyone has a photo of Derek in hand and knows how clever and skilled he is. We won't underestimate him."

"What about you?" Claire asked Wolf.

He checked his watch, not looking the least bit tired. "I'll be in the gym. I need to burn off some energy."

Of course he did. While she was falling apart, he was perfectly calm and confident.

It shouldn't annoy her. But it did.

"Come on," Vivi said, heading for the exit. "Let's get you back to your room."

Claire didn't argue. She was too tired to argue. Too tired to think. Too tired to do anything but follow Vivi down the corridor to her room.

"Try to sleep," Vivi said. "Tomorrow's going to be a long day."

But sleep was impossible.

Claire lay in bed, staring at the ceiling, her mind racing. Derek had been in her apartment. Had touched her phone. Had installed spyware and watched her for months. Had known where she lived, where she worked, who she talked to.

Had known about Lily. Had maybe been there the night Lily died. The thought made her sick.

She sat up, checked the time. She'd been lying here for nearly two hours, and sleep felt impossible.

Grabbing a sweatshirt, she pulled it on over her tank top. Maybe walking would help. Maybe moving would quiet her brain.

Bobcat jumped to attention when she emerged. "Everything okay?"

Security lights cast long shadows. She could hear the hum of electronics from the ops room, the distant sound of someone typing—probably Lynx, who seemed never to sleep.

"Can I use the gym?"

His brows drew down. "Let me clear it with the Commander." He spoke into his radio quietly, then nodded when Wolf's voice responded. "You're good to go."

Claire followed him, hoping against hope that Wolf was still there. She needed to get away. Away from the lifeless, generic room. Away from her spinning thoughts.

They arrived at the gym. The door was cracked open, light spilling into the hallway. And inside—

Wolf.

He was hitting a heavy bag with brutal efficiency. No gloves—just bare fists and controlled fury. His shirt was discarded on the floor, his upper body slick with sweat. Every punch landed with precision, the bag swinging on its chain.

Claire should leave, should go back to her room. She should not stand here watching him work out his demons.

But she couldn't move. Because she recognized what she was seeing. It wasn't just exercise. It wasn't just blowing off steam.

It was rage. Pure, controlled, barely contained rage.

He hit the bag again and again. Hard enough that his knuckles were bleeding.

"You're going to break your hands," Claire said, walking in.

Wolf froze mid-punch. Turned. His eyes locked on hers, and for a moment, she saw something raw in his expression. Something that looked like pain.

Then it was gone. Professional distance sliding back into place.

"Couldn't sleep?" His voice was steady, controlled, like he hadn't just been beating a bag bloody.

"No." Claire stepped into the gym. "You?"

"Don't need much."

"Because you're superhuman?"

He grabbed a towel and wiped his face. "What are you doing here, Claire?"

Bobcat stood at the door. "Should I stay?"

Wolf waved him off. "It's fine. I've got her. Go grab some sleep."

The man disappeared.

Claire tried not to ogle his ripped abs and defined chest. "I don't know. Walking. Thinking. Trying not to think." She moved closer. "What are you doing? Besides destroying your hands?"

"Training."

"That's not training. That's punishment."

His jaw tightened. "It's late. You should get some rest."

"So should you."

"I'm fine."

"You're bleeding." Claire gestured to his knuckles. "And you've been down here for hours."

Wolf looked at his hands like he'd forgotten about them. Blood smeared across his knuckles, mixing with sweat. "It's nothing," he said.

"Don't be that guy." Claire crossed to him and took his hand. Examined the torn skin. "You need to clean this. Bandage it."

"I've had worse."

"I'm sure you have, but that doesn't mean you should ignore it."

She was still holding his hand. Standing close enough to feel the heat radiating off his body. Close enough to see the tension in his jaw, the way his chest rose and fell with his breathing.

"Why are you really down here?" he asked quietly.

Claire looked up at him, at this man who'd protected her, pushed her, kissed her. Who carried secrets like armor. "Every time I close my eyes, I see Derek's face, and I keep thinking—" Her voice cracked. "He was stalking me. Watching me. Pretending to be my friend." She shuddered again, disgusted. "I feel so stupid. Defiled."

"And he's gloating right now because that's exactly what he wants."

"You think he knows we've figured out who he is?"

"Yes. That's why he left work abruptly without so much as an excuse."

Tears burned behind her eyes. Angry tears. "He's turned Lily's death into a mockery. How did I not see it? How did I not know?"

"Predators are good at hiding." Garrett's free hand came up and cupped her face. "You couldn't have known."

"You keep saying that."

"Because it's true."

Claire closed her eyes, leaned into his touch. "I feel like I'm losing my mind."

"You're not. You're processing trauma."

"You sound like Vivi."

"Doc is smart."

Claire opened her eyes. Wolf was watching her with an intensity that made her breath catch. His thumb brushed her cheekbone, wiping away a tear she hadn't realized had fallen.

"You're not alone in this," he said quietly. "You know that, right?"

"I know." Her voice was barely a whisper. "But sometimes it feels like I am. Like I'm the only one who's falling apart while everyone else just keeps going."

"You're not falling apart. You're holding together despite everything trying to break you. That's strength, not weakness."

"Is that what you're doing?" Claire gestured to the punching bag, to his bleeding hands. "Holding together?"

Something flickered in his eyes. Something that looked like recognition. "Yeah," he said. "That's exactly what I'm doing."

They stood there, breathing the same air. His hand was still on her face. Her hand still held his bloody knuckles.

"I should go," she said, her voice coming out low and rough.

But she didn't move.

"Probably," he said.

"You should get some rest."

"So should you."

Neither of them moved.

"Wolf, what is your—?"

"Don't," he said softly. "Don't ask me questions I can't answer right now."

"Can't or won't?"

"Both."

Claire wanted to be angry. Wanted to demand answers. Wanted to know why he kept holding back when everything else between them felt so...real.

But she was too tired. Too raw. Too desperate for comfort to push him away.

"Will you walk me back to my room?" she asked instead.

"I wasn't about to let you go alone. Let me clean up a minute." He locked the door to the gym, then disappeared into the changing room. She heard the shower come on.

A few minutes later, he reemerged, hair wet, knuckles professionally wrapped like he'd bandaged himself up dozens of times. He smelled like pine and sandalwood. Smiled at her as he unlocked the door and led her out.

They walked in silence. The compound was quiet, everyone else asleep or on patrol. Just the two of them and the shadows. At her door, Claire stopped. Turned. "I know I keep saying this, but thank you," she said. "For everything. Not just for keeping me safe, but for pushing me when I needed it. For..." She trailed off. *For kissing me. For making me feel alive again. For being someone I could fall for if I let myself.*

"You don't have to thank me," Garrett said. "It's my job."

"Yeah, your job. Is that all I am to you? A job?"

He didn't deny it. Didn't confirm it. Just looked at her with those green eyes that saw too much. "Get some sleep, Claire."

"Are you staying?"

He nodded. Dropped his bag beside the door and leaned on the wall. "I'm staying."

"Wolf?"

"Yeah?"

"Whatever you're punishing yourself for, it's not your fault either."

His expression turned flat. He opened her door. "Goodnight, Claire."

Inside, she deflated, disappointed he hadn't let her ask her questions. He had a wall so high and thick that she wondered if anyone could get through it. What secrets did he carry? What guilt drove him to bloody his hands on a punching bag for hours?

More worrisome, why did she feel like she knew him despite knowing almost nothing about him at all?

Her thoughts spun. Her feet wouldn't stop moving. She kept seeing him in the gym, his muscles flexing, his fists beating the bag, everything about him solid and strong and unforgiving.

Her fingers touched her lips. Her body ached for his touch. He might exorcise his demons in the gym, but she needed something entirely different.

She'd built a career on taking calculated risks. Trusted her instincts as much as she'd trusted her training. And right now, her instincts were screaming. There was one sure-fire way to clear her head.

Yanking open the door, she saw Wolf's brows hit his hairline right before she pulled him into her room and kissed him.

CHAPTER ELEVEN

Garrett had been leaning against the wall outside Claire's door, trying to convince himself he could spend the night on guard without thinking about kissing her again.

I should tell her everything. Admit the truth.

Then the door flew open, and as if she'd read his mind, Claire yanked him inside. In the next heartbeat, her mouth was on his.

He froze. Shock and desire warred in his chest. This was wrong. Her emotions were heightened because she was feeling vulnerable, and he was hiding an awful secret.

But as her mouth moved against his and her fingers wrapped around his neck, pulling him closer, desire won out.

His hands found her waist, her shirt riding up, exposing her skin. She tasted like mint toothpaste. Her fingers clenched his shirt, holding on like he was the only thing keeping her from floating away.

The door was still open behind him. Garrett kicked it shut without breaking the kiss. Every reason he shouldn't do this evaporated the moment her tongue swept against his.

He managed to pull back an inch. "Claire."

Her pupils were blown wide. "Don't you dare suggest I don't know what I'm doing. Tell me this isn't what you want, too."

She was so damn beautiful. "Of course I do. But you're exhausted. You've been through hell."

"And I might die at the hands of a serial killer." Her hands slid under his shirt, fingers splaying against his abs. "I want you. Unless you don't—"

He kissed her. Hard. Claiming. Because not wanting her was impossible.

She'd been in his head since the moment Vivi had shown him her photo. Every wall he'd built had started crumbling the second he'd met her in person. Now, with her hands on his skin and her body pressed against his, those walls didn't just crumble.

They shattered.

He walked her back toward the bed, never breaking the kiss. The back of her knees hit the mattress and she sat, looking at him with an expression that was equal parts vulnerable and determined.

"Last chance to stop," he said. His voice was rough, barely controlled. "Because if we do this, everything changes."

"Will you get fired?"

"Probably." He grinned. "It'll be worth it."

"Then we do this." Claire's hands went to the hem of her sweatshirt. She pulled it off in one smooth motion, revealing the tank top underneath. "Stop trying to protect me from my own choices, Wolf."

Wolf. Not Garrett. Not Bobby.

The reminder should have stopped him. Should have made him confess everything before this went any further. But she was reaching for him again, pulling him down to her, and he was too weak to resist.

He'd tell her tomorrow. After Derek was caught. After she was safe. After he could look her in the eye and explain why he'd kept the secret.

Tonight, he'd be selfish. Tonight, he'd take what she was offering and try not to think about how badly this would hurt when the truth came out.

His mouth found hers again, softer this time. Less desperate. More deliberate. He wanted to memorize this. The way she tasted. The small sound she made when his teeth grazed her lower lip. The way her hands gripped his shoulders as if she was afraid he'd disappear.

"Tell me what you need," he murmured against her mouth.

"You." Her fingers slid into his hair. "Just you."

He kissed her jaw, down her throat. Found the spot where her pulse hammered and lingered there. Her head fell back, giving him access, trusting him completely.

The trust nearly broke him. "Claire." Her name was half prayer, half apology.

"Stop overthinking." Her hands found the hem of his

shirt and tugged it upward. "I can feel you thinking. Just...be here. With me."

He helped her remove his shirt, let her explore. Her fingers traced the scars on his ribs, his shoulder. Evidence of missions gone wrong, of being too slow or too reckless or too focused on saving someone else to protect himself.

"You've been hurt," she said quietly.

"Occupational hazard."

"Does it hurt now?"

"No." Nothing hurt now except the knowledge that she didn't know who he really was.

Her hands moved lower, traced his abs, the V of muscle that disappeared beneath his jeans. Her touch was confident but not aggressive. Exploring. Learning him.

"Your turn," Garrett said.

Her tank top joined his shirt on the floor. She wasn't wearing a bra. Of course, she wasn't. She'd been trying to sleep when she'd decided to find him.

His breath caught. She was all soft curves and smooth skin and trust in her eyes.

"You're staring," Claire said, but she didn't cover herself. Didn't hide.

"Yeah." His voice was rough. "I am."

He lowered her back onto the bed and followed her down. Kissed her again while his hands mapped territory he'd been dreaming about for days. The curve of her waist. The dip of her spine. The soft swell of her breasts.

She arched into his touch, made a sound that shot straight through him. Tonight wasn't about guilt. Tonight was about her. About giving her comfort and pleasure, and the connection she needed.

He could hate himself tomorrow.

His mouth moved lower to kiss the underside of one breast. Her sternum. Her ribs. She trembled beneath him, her fingers tangled in his hair.

"You're killing me," she breathed.

"Good." He looked up, saw her eyes dark with desire. "That's the idea."

She rocked her hips under him. He removed her pants, then his. As he knelt between her legs, he said, "Tell me what you need, sweetheart. Use your words."

Her cheeks flushed. "More. I need more."

He gave her more. Kissed lower, made her gasp. Her hips lifted off the bed, and he held her steady, took his time, drove her higher. When she shattered, his name on her lips, Garrett felt something in his chest crack open. Something he'd kept locked away for all these years.

This. This was what he'd been missing. Not just physical pleasure, but connection. Real connection with someone who saw him—even if she didn't know all of him.

Claire pulled him back up, kissed him like she was drowning and he was air. Her hands fumbled with his underwear, tugging them down. He helped, kicking them off.

"Condom?" she asked breathlessly.

"Wallet."

"Of course you're prepared."

"Navy SEAL. Always prepared for any outcome."

She laughed. Actually laughed. And the sound was so unexpected, so perfect, that Garrett had to kiss her again just to taste her joy.

He retrieved the condom and dealt with it quickly. When he settled between her thighs, Claire's hands framed his face.

"Hey," she said softly. "You still with me?"

"Yeah." He kissed her palm. "I'm with you."

"Then stop holding back. I won't break."

"I know you won't." Because she was the strongest person he knew. "But I might."

Her expression softened. "Then break. I've got you."

And somehow, impossibly, he believed her.

When he finally pushed inside, Claire's breath hitched. Her fingers dug into his shoulders, holding on. He stilled, gave her time to adjust, watched her face. "Okay?" he asked.

"Better than okay." She rolled her hips experimentally, and Garrett groaned. "Move. Please."

He did. Slow at first, letting her set the pace. But she urged him faster, deeper, her legs wrapping around his waist. Her short nails dug into his back, and her teeth grazed his neck.

They found a rhythm that was both familiar and entirely new, like they'd done this before. Like they were meant to fit together exactly like this. Claire's breath came in gasps. Garrett buried his face in her neck, breathed her in—vanilla shampoo and sweat and something indefinably her. His hands gripped her hips, angled her just right, and she cried out.

"That's it," he murmured against her skin. "Let go."

"Not without you."

"Claire—"

"Together," she insisted. Her hand slid between them, and the added pressure made his vision go white.

They fell together. Shattered together. Held on to each other like the world was ending and this was all that mattered.

Maybe it was.

Afterward, they lay tangled in sheets that smelled like sex and Claire's soap. Garrett's heart was still racing, his breathing unsteady. Claire curled against his side, her head on his chest, one leg thrown over his.

"That was..." she started.

"Yeah."

"Are you always this articulate post-sex?"

He laughed. "Only with you."

Claire propped herself up on one elbow and looked down at him. Her hair was a mess. Her lips were swollen. She'd never looked more beautiful. "Can I ask you something?" she said.

Garrett tensed. "Depends on the question."

"Why did you really take this mission? And don't say it's just your job."

His chest tightened because he couldn't tell her the truth. Not yet. But he couldn't lie to her either. Not after this.

"Because when I saw your file," he said carefully, "when I read about what you'd survived, what you'd overcome...I knew I had to help. You reminded me of someone I lost. Someone I couldn't save."

"Your sister."

"She deserved an older brother who could protect her." The truth and the lie were all mixed together.

Claire's expression softened. "Is that why you're so good at this? At pushing me when I need it? Because you understand the guilt?"

"Maybe." Probably. "Or maybe I just recognize strength when I see it."

She smiled. Leaned down and kissed him. Soft. Sweet. Nothing like the desperate passion from earlier.

"I can't stop saying it...thank you," she whispered against his mouth.

"For what?"

"For seeing me. Not just the FBI agent, the victim, or the survivor. But me."

Garrett's throat was tight. She was thanking him for something he didn't deserve. He wasn't seeing all of her. He was seeing CJ, Lily's best friend. The other girl he'd failed to protect fifteen years ago.

But he couldn't say that. So instead, he pulled her closer, kissed her again, and tried to memorize every detail of this moment before it all fell apart.

They slept, and when he woke to her hands exploring him beneath the covers, he made love to her again. Slower this time. More tender. He took his time, learned what made her gasp, what made her moan, what made her say his name like a prayer.

When they finally collapsed, exhausted and sated,

Claire fell asleep almost immediately. The stress and trauma of the past days finally caught up with her.

Garrett lay awake, watching her sleep. She was curled on her side, facing him. One hand was carefully tucked under her cheek. Her breathing was deep and even. Peaceful for the first time since she'd arrived.

And all he could think was: *I'm going to lose her.*

Not to Derek. He'd make damn sure Derek never touched her. But to the truth. To the Bobby revelation. To the knowledge that he'd been lying to her from the start.

She'd hate him. And she'd have every right to.

He reached out and brushed a strand of hair from her face. She didn't stir. He was both glad and disappointed.

He'd told Vivi he'd tell her after Derek was caught. But now, lying here with her next to him, he wondered if that was just another excuse. Another way to delay the inevitable. Because the truth was, he didn't want to lose this. Didn't want to lose her. And once she knew who he really was, everything would change.

I'm sorry, CJ, he thought. *I'm sorry I'm too much of a coward to tell you the truth.*

But tomorrow—tomorrow he'd catch Derek and then sit her down and explain everything. Tomorrow he'd face whatever came.

In the final hours before dawn, he'd just hold her and pretend they had forever.

GARRETT WOKE to sunlight streaming through the window and Claire's warm body pressed against his. She was still asleep, her hair spread across the pillow, one arm draped over his chest.

He checked his watch—0743 hours. The meeting at the police station was at ten. They had time.

Not enough, though. Never enough.

Claire stirred, made a slight sound. Her eyes fluttered open, unfocused for a moment. Then she saw him and smiled. "Hey," she said, voice rough with sleep.

"Hey, yourself."

"Did you sleep?"

"Some." More than he usually got. "I shirked my bodyguard duties, though."

Claire stretched, chuckled. "I'd say you were as close to me as you could get. Your protection service is first-rate."

He pinched her side playfully, and she let out a little yelp. She propped herself up, the sheet slipping. "We should probably talk about this."

Garrett's chest tightened. "Yeah, we probably should."

"I don't regret it," she said quickly. "But I know this complicates things. Just...don't turn this into a guilt trip, okay? We're two professionals. Adults. We knew what we were doing."

He kissed her. "I don't regret it either, and yes, it complicates things. But we'll figure it out."

"After Derek's caught?"

He glanced up at the ceiling, rubbing a circle on her shoulder with his thumb. "After Derek's caught." *And after I tell you who I really am and watch you walk away.*

Claire studied his face. "You're holding something back."

His heart stopped. "What?"

"I can see it in your eyes. There's always something you're not telling me." She touched his face. "You don't want to tell me your name—fine, I get it. Shadow Point Security has rules about client-bodyguard interaction. But it's more than that, isn't it? This place, this job...it's armor you hide behind. Eventually, I need to know all of you. Not just the parts you think are safe to share."

Garrett's throat was tight. "I know. After this is over, I'll tell you everything. I promise."

He could live with that compromise even if Vivi wouldn't approve.

Claire seemed to accept his decision. She brushed her lips over his, soft and sweet. "Okay. But I'm holding you to that promise."

"I know you will."

They showered together—which turned into more touching and kissing—before reluctantly getting dressed. Claire tugged on fresh jeans and an FBI t-shirt. Garrett wore tactical pants and a Shadow Point polo.

Ready for the meeting. Pretending last night hadn't happened.

Except it had. And Garrett could see it in the way Claire looked at him. In the small smile she tried to hide. In the way her hand brushed his when they walked down the hallway.

In the ops room, the team was already assembled. Lynx was at his laptop. Grizzly was checking weapons and Hawk was reviewing tactical maps. Bobcat was on perimeter duty.

Vivi informed him that her husband, Lt. Commander Ian Kincaid, had joined the team. "He's also a former SEAL and works for our sister company, Shadow Force International. He's on loan to help us out." She gestured toward the monitors. "Currently, he's walking the compound with Bobcat, reviewing entry and exit points."

Vivi studied Garrett, and he saw the knowing look in her eyes. Nothing got past her. She knew exactly where he'd spent the night.

Great.

"Sleep well?" she asked. "Coffee's fresh."

"Thanks, Doc," Garrett said, pouring two cups. He handed one to Claire, who wrapped her hands around it gratefully.

"I haven't slept that well in ages," Claire told Vivi, that small smile teasing the corners of her mouth.

"Status?" Garrett asked quickly, trying to change the subject.

"The FBI team from Missoula should arrive at the station in about ninety minutes," Lynx reported. "Local PD is coordinating with them and us, but they seem relieved to turn this over to the Feds. There's no sign of Sullivan anywhere. It's like he vanished."

"He's here," Claire said quietly. "Somewhere close. He's waiting."

Garrett didn't doubt her instincts. "We proceed as planned—a full briefing at the station where we coordinate with the FBI and the local PD."

The next hour played out according to plan.

Garrett met Ian and liked him immediately. He'd just gotten back to the States from Bolivia and was jet-lagged. The tall man with pine green eyes that didn't miss anything kissed his wife's head and left them to grab a shower. "I'll meet you at the station once I've cleaned up," he said to Garrett.

They all ate breakfast and then prepared to leave. "I'm going to stop at the crime scene," Vivi said as they walked to the parking lot. "I want to get a look at where Derek killed Ms. Martinez, take a few pictures, and document what I see to put into Trident. The more information my system has, the better. It won't take long. I'll meet you at the station."

They took three different vehicles—Vivi in her Lexus, Garrett and Claire in a black SUV loaded with tech and weapons, and a third vehicle with Lynx and Grizzly bringing up the rear.

The streets of Blackridge were moderately busy, with folks heading to work and dropping off kids at school.

Claire studied it. "This is a lovely town," she said. "I can only imagine how they're reeling from this tragedy."

Garrett reached over and squeezed her hand. "Places like this feel safe until they don't. But we're going to catch Derek, and when we do, they'll feel safe again."

The station was a small, cinder-block building with a wide front entrance and a pitched roof. A flag flew proudly on a pole in the postage-stamp-sized yard. They parked, Garrett insisting Claire stay in the vehicle until he came to get her. Lynx and Grizzly joined him, and the three moved as a unit to surround her as they guided her inside.

Just as they crossed the threshold, Ian arrived. He jogged up the steps and nodded at Garrett. "Hope you don't mind if I tag along."

Detective Mills with Blackridge PD greeted them and took them into a conference room. "Special Agent Dawson, it's nice to meet you. Wish it were under better circumstances."

Claire shook the man's hand, and Ian introduced himself, then Garrett and the others as simply the 'Shadow Point Security Team.' No real names, not even their call signs. "Dr. Montgomery will be here shortly," he told the detective.

Coffee was offered, and the FBI team from Missoula showed up. More introductions. Once those were done, Special Agent Honoree Hendricks took charge. She gave all of them a quick briefing, then turned the floor over to Claire. "We've all read your reports, Agent Dawson. Now, we'd like to hear directly from you. Tell us what we need to know about Derek Sullivan in order to stop him."

"Should we wait for Dr. Montgomery?" Claire asked Garrett.

He glanced at Ian. "Call her? She should be here by now, shouldn't she?"

Ian took out his phone and dialed. After a minute, he frowned. "It keeps going to voicemail."

Garrett's blood ran cold. "Lynx, you got a tracker on her?"

Lynx's fingers flew over his keyboard. "Her car's still at the coffee shop."

Ian stood. "I'll check on her. She's probably lost track of the time."

As he left, Claire straightened her blazer and addressed the gathered group. "Derek Brands, aka Derek Sullivan, is coming afte me because i's personal," she said, and proceeded for the next few minutes to explain why.

Questions were asked and answered. Claire called on Garrett to share the plan they'd come up with to bait Derek and trap him. Standing beside her at the head of the conference table, he felt a renewed kinship with her. They were equals, partners, in more ways than one.

Just as Garrett was finishing up, Ian rushed in. "She's gone," he said without preamble.

The room fell quiet. Garrett's eyes met Claire's. She paled.

"Say that again," Garrett said, his voice deadly calm.

A muscle in Ian's jaw jumped. "Dr. Montgomery—my wife—is missing."

CHAPTER TWELVE

The conference room erupted into chaos.

Ian stood frozen in the doorway, his face a mask of controlled fury. "Her car's at the coffee shop. The driver's door is open, and her purse is on the ground. No sign of struggle, but I just received this text." He held up his phone. "*You can't hide from me, Claire.*"

Claire's stomach dropped. Vivi. *Derek had taken Vivi.*

"Lynx, pull traffic cams," Wolf barked. "Hawk, get to high ground, eyes on the town. Grizzly, secure the perimeter here. Everyone else, lock down this location."

The team moved instantly, years of training overriding shock. Detective Mills was already on the radio, coordinating with his officers. Special Agent Hendricks grabbed her phone.

Claire couldn't move. Couldn't breathe. This was her fault. Derek had taken Vivi because of her. Another person in danger. Another person who might die because the Countdown Killer wanted to kill her.

"Claire." Wolf's hand was on her shoulder. "I need you to focus."

"He has Vivi because of me."

"He has Vivi because he's a predator." His voice was stern. "And we're going to get her back."

Ian crossed to Lynx's laptop, looked over his shoulder at the feeds. "Anything?"

"Traffic cams in Blackridge are sparse," Lynx said, fingers flying. "But look here." He pointed to a grainy image. "Black van, no plates, heading north on Mountain Road. Timestamp puts it ten minutes after Vivi would have arrived at the coffee shop."

"Can you track it?" Ian's voice was deadly calm. Too calm.

"Trying. But Mountain Road splits into three different routes. If he went off-road..." Lynx trailed off.

They all knew what that meant. Derek could be anywhere.

Claire forced herself to think. To profile. Derek was smart. Methodical. He'd been planning this for months. Maybe years. She'd thrown him a curveball coming to Montana, and he was escalating since he couldn't get to her. First, by killing Rebecca Martinez, now by taking Vivi.

"He's going to make contact," Claire said.

Everyone turned to look at her.

"He took Vivi, rather than killing her on the spot, to draw me out," she continued. "He wants me to know he has her. He'll make demands."

"How soon?" Wolf asked.

The anniversary of Lily's death was today. "Today," Claire said. "The longer he waits, the more time we have to find him, and he wants to stick to his original timeline."

As if on cue, Lynx's computer chimed. "Incoming message, routed through multiple servers." He pulled it up on the main screen.

A photo appeared of Vivi, bound to a chair in what looked like a cabin. Her face was pale but defiant. A gag covered her mouth. Behind her was darkness and rough wooden walls. Below the photo was text that read:

Claire comes to me. Alone. Two hours. Coordinates below. Or Dr. Montgomery dies the way Lily did.

Claire's blood ran cold. The coordinates appeared. "That's deep in the mountains north of town," Wolf said. His eyes cut to Lynx. "Trace it," he ordered.

"Already on it," Lynx said. "He's bouncing the signal through... Commander, this is NSA-level encryption. He's good."

"He's a former Navy electronics tech," Claire said. "He knows how to hide."

Ian was studying the photo, his jaw working. "That cabin. It's remote, off-grid."

"We have two hours," Detective Mills said. "We can get search teams—"

"It's my cabin," Wolf said, and everyone stopped. "He's making this personal for me, too. He expects me to show up."

"No." Claire's voice was clear. Certain. "He's expecting me. He wants me, not you. If I don't go, he kills her."

"Absolutely not," Wolf said. His tone left no room for argument.

Claire turned to face him. "This works with your plan, don't you see? I have to go. We don't have a choice."

"There's always a choice. And the choice is not sending you into a trap alone."

"I'm an FBI agent. I've been trained for exactly this kind of—"

"You're the target!" Wolf's voice echoed through the room. "He wants you dead, Claire. That's the entire point of this. Vivi is bait. And he's thumbing his nose at me."

"I know that." Claire kept her voice level. "Which is why I'm the only one who can do this. He'll be watching for a tactical team, for you. But me, alone? That's what he wants. That's what I'll give him."

"And then what?" Wolf demanded. "He kills you like he killed Lily? He'll kill Vivi, too, just like he killed four other women. That's your plan?"

Claire stepped closer, lowered her voice so only he could hear. "My plan is to trust you. To trust your team. You'll be there. But Derek can't know that. He has to believe I'm following his orders."

"Claire—"

"Vivi has been nothing but kind to me. Helpful. Now, she's in danger because of me." Claire's voice cracked. "I won't let another person die because Derek Sullivan is obsessed with me."

Wolf's hands clenched into fists. Every line of his

body radiated tension, barely contained fury. "There has to be another way."

"There isn't, and you know it."

For a long moment, they glared at each other. Claire could see the war in his eyes—the commander who knew she was right versus the man who'd just spent the night making love to her.

Finally, Ian spoke. "She's right, Commander."

Wolf turned to him. "Ian—"

"She's right," Ian repeated. His voice was steady despite the fact that his wife was the hostage. "Sullivan won't move until he sees Claire, but that doesn't mean she goes in unprotected."

Wolf blew out a heavy breath. He looked at Claire. "You'll wear a wire and a tracker. We'll fit you with a vest under your shirt."

"He'll search me," Claire said.

"Then we make sure it's good enough that he won't find it," Lynx said. He was already pulling equipment from cases. "I've got a tracker that goes under the skin. It's temporary and bioabsorbable. It will dissolve in seventy-two hours, but it'll work for today."

"And the wire?" Wolf asked. His voice was tight.

"Embedded in her bra." Lynx held up a device no bigger than a button. "Audio only, but it'll transmit everything within a fifty-foot radius."

Wolf studied the equipment, then glanced at Claire. "And if he finds the tracker? When he knows we're coming?"

"I'll hold him off until you get there," Claire said.

The next hour was a blur of preparation. Lynx injected the tracker into Claire's left shoulder blade. It stung, but she barely felt it through the adrenaline. The wire was sewn into her bra. The FBI team coordinated with Mills to establish a perimeter around the area in case Derek Sullivan tried to escape.

Wolf stood in the corner of the small office they'd commandeered, watching. His expression was unreadable, but Claire could feel the tension radiating off him.

"Vest," Ian said, holding out tactical body armor.

Claire shook her head. "Too obvious. He'll search me and find it. He'll know you're setting him up."

Wolf took the vest and pressed it to her chest. "He expects us to do exactly that. We play into his game, remember?"

She hesitated. "It's risky."

"If Vivi were here, she'd go with reverse psychology like the Commander is suggesting," Ian said. "Serial killers get cocky after so many successful kills. I've heard her say it dozens of times. He'll expect you to wear a vest and have a wire. When he finds them, all you have to do is seem surprised that he's so damn smart. Make him feel more intelligent than you."

"The cabin is forty minutes north," Hawk said, studying a topographical map. "Remote. Heavy tree cover. Limited approach vectors. I can get a shot from here." He pointed to a ridge about fifty yards from the cabin location. "But you'll have to get him near a front window or outside. It'll be tight."

"Take it," Wolf ordered. "Ian, Grizzly—you're

ground support. Stay concealed, move in when Claire makes contact."

"And you?" Claire asked.

His eyes met hers. "I'll be close. Always."

They drove in separate vehicles: Claire in a Bureau sedan, alone. Hawk and Grizzly in one tactical vehicle, taking a different route to approach from the east. Garrett, Ian, and Lynx in another, circling west.

The communications system crackled to life in Claire's ear. Lynx had given her the tiniest receiver she'd ever seen. It was nearly invisible.

"Radio check," Lynx's voice said. "Paperclip?"

God, she hated that call sign. "It's Fury," she corrected. Her hands were steady on the wheel, but her heart was racing. "I'm twenty minutes out."

"Copy....Fury." Was that a smile she heard in his tone? "Hawk is in position on the ridge and has a visual on the cabin. One vehicle outside, which confirms our target's location."

"Any sign of Derek?" Claire asked.

"Just the van, but there's no movement in the surrounding area. He's no doubt inside."

Claire's throat was tight. She was driving toward a man who wanted to kill her. Who'd spent years planning it. Who'd murdered at least four women—maybe five, if Vivi didn't survive. Who'd possibly been there the night Lily died.

Her hands tightened on the wheel. *Focus on the anger, not the fear.* Wolf's voice in her head. *Get angry.*

She *was* angry. Furious. Derek Sullivan had

destroyed her sense of safety. Had invaded her privacy for months. Had taken Vivi—a woman who'd done nothing but try to help.

Her cell phone rang. The ID read *Wolf*. He was staying off the comms so the others wouldn't hear.

"Claire." His voice instantly calmed her. "You don't have to do this."

"Yes, I do."

"I can't lose you." His voice cracked slightly. "Not after last night. Not after..."

"You won't lose me." Her voice was steady. "I'm coming back. We both are."

A pause. "I'm holding you to that."

"I know."

The cabin appeared through the trees. Small, weathered, isolated. No other structures for miles. The black van sat outside, empty.

Claire parked fifty yards away, as instructed in Derek's message. She breathed in for four counts, held it, breathed out. Killed the engine. "In position," she said quietly.

"Copy," Wolf's voice. "We're already in position. Hawk has overwatch. You're not alone."

"I know." But it felt like she was. Felt like she was fourteen again, walking into a nightmare. She opened the car door and stepped out. The mountain air was cold, pine-scented. Peaceful.

She purposefully did the breathing exercise again, thinking about Wolf out here. It was peaceful, but... lonely, too.

Her chest had a mind of its own. She couldn't draw a deep breath. She'd confronted killers before. Walked into dangerous situations. This time was different. This time, it was personal.

The cabin door opened before she reached it. Derek Sullivan stood in the doorway. The monster. "Claire." His voice was warm, friendly, just like it had been all those times at work. "Right on time. I knew you'd come. We've both been waiting for this, haven't we?"

A lump formed in her throat. Her legs turned to jelly. "Where's Dr. Montgomery?"

"Inside. Alive for now." He gestured. "Come in. We have so much to talk about."

Claire didn't move. "Let me see her first."

Derek smiled. "You're not in a position to make demands. But..." He stepped aside.

Through the doorway, Claire could see Vivi bound to a chair and gagged. Her eyes were alert. She jerked her chin toward something on the other side of the open door. Blinked twice.

"Satisfied?" Derek asked. "Now, get inside, or I'll slash her throat." He flashed a hunting knife.

All the air whooshed out of her lungs. But Claire walked forward past Derek and into the cabin. The door closed behind her with a sound like a tomb sealing.

The cabin was small. One room, mostly. A kitchenette in one corner. A jacket hung on a hook near the door. Wood was stacked in the small fireplace. The chair where Vivi sat was in the center. Nearby was a table with rope and zip ties.

Vivi's eyes darted to the right again. Claire turned and froze. Photographs—dozens of them—were taped to the walls.

All of Claire.

Claire at her apartment. At the Bureau. At the grocery store. At a restaurant with colleagues. Photos spanning months. Maybe years. Her entire life, documented. Watched. Stalked.

"Impressive, isn't it?" Derek said behind her. He locked the door. "Five years of work. Five years of getting close and earning your trust. Watching you live your life, completely oblivious."

Claire forced herself to look at him. "Why?"

"Why?" He laughed, sounding amused. "You really don't know? You're the one who saw too much and lived when she shouldn't have. He was obsessed with you, Claire. And when the police killed him..."

"You decided to finish what he started," Claire said.

"I decided to make you pay." Derek circled her slowly. "You took my cousin from me. The only family I had. He was brilliant, powerful. And you—a scared little girl—got him killed."

She stepped closer to Vivi. "He got himself killed. He murdered Lily."

"Lily was collateral damage." Derek's voice was cold. "She wasn't the target. You were, Claire. You were always the point."

Claire's blood ran cold. "What?"

"Collin was hunting *you* that night," Derek said. "Lily was just there, in the way. If she hadn't been with you..." He shrugged. "But she was. She didn't fight, so she died, and you lived. And that wasn't right. Collin couldn't fix it, so I will."

Vivi made a sound behind the gag, struggling against the restraints.

"Oh, Dr. Montgomery wants to contribute." Derek walked to Vivi, yanked the gag down. "Go ahead. Tell Claire how this is going to end."

Vivi's eyes met Claire's. "It's a trap. He knows the team is here. He—"

Derek backhanded her. Vivi's head snapped to the side.

"That's enough." He replaced the gag. Turned back to Claire. "She's right, of course. I knew you wouldn't come alone. I'm not stupid. Your precious Shadow Point Security is out there somewhere, thinking they're going to save you."

He pulled a device from his pocket. Small. Digital. A trigger. "But I've been planning this for a long time," Derek continued. "And I always have a backup plan."

Claire's heart stopped. "What did you do?"

"The police station. Such a nice building. Shame about the gas leak." Derek smiled. "Or what will look like a gas leak. Really, it's C-4. Not much. Just enough to level the building and kill everyone inside."

"You're blowing up the police station?" Claire couldn't breathe.

"In..." Derek checked his watch. "Five minutes. Unless you convince your team to stand down. To let this happen. You and me, Claire. The way it's supposed to be."

Through her earpiece—silent since she'd entered the cabin—she heard Wolf's voice, tight with fury. "We heard him. Lynx, can you disarm remotely?"

"Negative," Lynx's voice. "He's air-gapped it. We need physical access."

"Then someone needs to get there," Wolf ordered. "Mills—evacuate the station. Now."

Derek was watching her face. "They're scrambling now, aren't they? I assume you're wired. So predictable."

He moved fast. Grabbed Claire's arm, yanked her forward. His hand ripped open her windbreaker, tore at her shirt. His hands found the tactical vest. "Really? You thought I wouldn't check?" He ripped it off and threw it across the room, leaving her in her tank top only.

Claire fought back, sending a knee to his groin and an elbow to his face. Her training and instincts made her dangerous, but Derek was trained, too. He absorbed the hits and slammed her against the wall. Her ears rang.

He caressed her cheek, then he shoved Claire into a chair next to Vivi and zip-tied her hands behind her back.

"Now," he said, sitting on the edge of the table, the knife in his hand. "Let me tell you about the night Lily died."

Claire's pulse hammered. "I was there."

"You *were* there, but you didn't see everything." Derek spun the knife. "Collin and I had been watching you for months. Young, pretty Claire Dawson. So trusting. So easy to track. We knew where you lived, where you went to school, who your friends were."

"Lily," Claire whispered.

"Yes, Lily Harper, your best friend. Also young and pretty. Also easy to grab when we found you two alone that night." Derek leaned forward. "Collin wanted you. But I convinced him—take the friend first. Make Claire watch. Make her feel powerless."

Tears burned in Claire's eyes. "You helped him."

"I was seventeen. Following my cousin. Learning." Derek's smile was cold. "But then you fought back and he was stupid, so stupid. He should have taken you both, but he didn't, not realizing you had his DNA under your nails. I was long gone by the time the cops came for him, but how sad he had to die, all because of you."

"He deserved to die."

"He chose death over prison. But that night when he killed Lily, he made me promise him something." Derek moved to crouch in front of her, twirling the knife handle in his palm. "*Find Claire. Make her pay. Finish what we started.*"

The knife traced her cheek. Not cutting—just reminding her how easily it could.

"So I changed my name," Derek continued. "Got clean. Joined the Navy. Learned skills. Got a job at the FBI after I tracked you down. And I waited. Watched. Planned." He stood, rubbed a strand of her hair between his fingers and thumb. "Five years, Claire. Five years of being patient. And now, finally, I get to keep my promise to Collin."

Through the window, Claire could see nothing. No sign of Wolf or the team. No sign of rescue. There was no noise on the comm, either.

There was only Derek, the knife, Vivi's terrified eyes, and the knowledge that time was almost up. The police station was about to explode. Had everyone gotten out?

Derek checked his watch. "Sixty seconds. Are you going to order your team to stand down?"

Claire met his eyes. "You're going to kill me anyway."

"True. But their deaths will be on your hands. There's no way they've already gotten everyone out. More people will die because of you." He gestured to Vivi. "I'm going to kill Dr. Montgomery first, make you watch like Collin planned to make you watch Lily..."

"Don't," Claire said, forcing authority into her tone like Wolf always did. Rage boiled in her veins. "Let her go. This is between us. Just you and me."

"It's always been between us," Derek agreed. "But killing is so much fun."

He moved toward Vivi, knife raised, his back to Claire. She had maybe three seconds before he slit Vivi's throat.

Not again.

The memory hit like a freight train—fourteen years old, hands bound, helpless while Collin Brands hurt Lily. The guilt that had poisoned fifteen years of her life.

But she wasn't that terrified girl anymore. She was a trained, skilled FBI agent. She'd spent all of her life making sure she'd never be helpless again.

And this time, she was going to fight.

This time, she would save an innocent person.

Claire made her choice.

CHAPTER THIRTEEN

Garrett crouched in the trees fifty yards from the cabin, every muscle coiled tight, listening to Derek Sullivan confess to murdering Lily.

I was seventeen. Following my cousin. Learning.

His hands clenched on his rifle. Derek had been there. Had convinced Collin to take Lily first. To make Claire watch.

Garrett's vision went red.

"Commander." Ian's voice in his ear, quiet but firm, as if the man knew his thoughts were spiraling. "Stay focused."

Garrett forced himself to breathe. To think tactically. Hawk was on the ridge, scope trained on the cabin. Ian and Grizzly were positioned east and west. Lynx was in one of the SUVs, coordinating with the Feds and Blackridge PD. Garrett had already heard him place a request for an ambulance.

Because there would be casualties.

And Claire was inside with a monster, zip-tied to a chair, listening to Derek describe how he'd helped murder her best friend.

"*Sixty seconds,*" Derek's voice came through Claire's wire. "*Are you going to order your team to stand down?*"

"Lynx," Garrett said into his comm. "Status on the station?"

"Evacuating now," Lynx's voice was tight. "But it's going to be close, Commander. Really close."

Forty-five seconds.

"*You're going to kill me anyway.*" Claire's voice. Steady despite everything.

"*True. But their deaths will be on your hands—*"

"Hawk," Garrett interrupted. "Do you have a shot?"

"Negative. He's moving too much. The risk of hitting Claire or Dr. Montgomery is too high."

Thirty seconds.

Through the cabin window, Garrett could see movement. Derek was standing and moving toward Vivi with the knife.

"*I'm going to kill Dr. Montgomery first, make you watch—*"

Ian cursed, and Garrett knew he was in motion, out of sight but ready to go in.

"*Don't,*" Claire's voice was surprisingly firm. Bitter. Angry. "*Let her go. This is between us.*"

"*It's always been between us. But killing is so much fun.*"

Twenty seconds.

Garrett was moving now, too, circling to the cabin's

blind side. Ian and Grizzly shifted positions, ready to breach on his signal.

"I've been looking forward to this for so long," Derek said. *"We're going to have such fun."*

Then Claire's voice, furious. "The fun is that you're too stupid to see it coming."

A crash. The sound of a chair splintering. Vivi screamed through the gag.

"Claire's moving!" Hawk's voice. "She's—shit, she headbutted him. He's down but getting up. She's trying to get free of the zip ties—"

Garrett ran.

THE ZIP TIES WERE TIGHT, but her hands were small. She'd been working them since he'd bound her, subtle movements he hadn't noticed while he monologued.

Almost loose. Not quite.

No time. Claire pushed off with her legs, stood despite her bound hands, and launched herself at him. All 130 pounds of her, shoulder-first, into his back.

They crashed into the table. The knife clattered away.

Derek spun faster than she anticipated. His fist caught her cheek, snapped her head back. Stars exploded across her vision. "You bitch," he snarled.

But Claire had trained for this. Trained for fighting with her hands bound, with limited mobility, with every-thing against her. She kicked his knee. Hard. Heard something pop. *For Lily. For Vivi. For every woman Derek and Collin have hurt.*

For the fourteen-year-old girl who couldn't fight back.

Derek howled, stumbled. His hand shot out, grabbed her hair. He yanked her down.

Claire twisted and brought her knee up into his groin. Once. Twice. He let go, gasping.

She rode the anger and the rage, a raw cry releasing from her throat. She scrambled toward the knife, but Derek grabbed her ankle, hauled her back. His weight landed on her, crushing. His hands found her throat.

"You should have died fifteen years ago," he gasped. "With Lily. I'm going to fix that now."

Claire couldn't breathe. Her vision darkened. She brought her bound hands up and slammed them into his throat.

Not enough. He squeezed harder.

From somewhere far away, she heard wood splintering. Shouting.

Derek's face above hers, twisted with rage. "Die," he whispered. "Finally *die*."

Then, suddenly, his weight was gone.

Wolf had hit Derek like a freight train. They crashed into the cabin wall decorated with her pictures. Wolf landed three punches before Derek recovered, twisted, and broke free.

"Commander!" Ian burst through the door behind him, weapon up.

Derek lunged for the knife. Wolf was faster. He

caught Derek's wrist, torqued it. Bone snapped and Derek screamed.

But he didn't stop. His other hand came up with another knife—a smaller one that had been hidden.

He slashed at Wolf's throat. Wolf jerked back. The blade caught his shoulder. Blood sprayed.

"Wolf!" Claire screamed.

Ian moved to intervene, but Derek kicked out, caught Ian's knee. The big man staggered.

Derek turned back to Wolf, knife raised. "You're too late. Just like you were too late for Lily. Right, Bobby?"

Wolf froze. Claire sucked in a breath. "What?" she managed to whisper.

Derek smiled at Wolf. There was blood on his teeth. "Oh yes. I know exactly who you are." He flicked his gaze at Claire, still zip-tied, still on the floor. "Does she know, Bobby? Does Claire know you're Lily's pathetic big brother? That you've been lying to her this whole time?"

Claire's world tilted.

Derek laughed. Actual laughter, wet and broken. "He didn't tell you? Shadow Point Security Commander Wolf is really Bobby Anderson. He goes by Garrett Cross these days, but he's Lily's half-brother. The one who wasn't there when she needed him. The one who's been lying to you since the moment you arrived."

"Claire—" Wolf started.

But Claire just blinked. "Bobby," she whispered. "You're *Bobby*?"

Derek used the distraction to lunge at Claire. It all

happened so fast. Wolf threw himself between them. The knife meant for Claire's heart caught him in the side.

He grunted, twisted, grabbed Derek's wrist. The knife fell.

Ian stood in front of Vivi, weapon trained on Derek. "Down! Get down now!"

Derek dropped to his knees, cradling his broken wrist. Still smiling. Still laughing.

"The truth is so very sweet, isn't it?" he said, sneering at Claire. "You and I will never be finished. You'll never forget me."

Wolf—Bobby, Garrett?—shoved Derek face-first onto the floor, securing his hands behind his back.

"Medic!" Ian called into his comm as he quickly cut Vivi loose. "We need medical inside the cabin. Officer wounded, suspect secured."

Garrett pressed his hand to his side. Blood seeped between his fingers. But when he moved toward Claire to help her up and free her restraints, he wouldn't look at her.

She stared at him, her head swimming like it had with her concussion. Everything blurred; her stomach twisted. Her body ached, but it was a distant throb compared to the agony in her heart.

"Claire," Wolf said. She couldn't yet think of him as anything else. "Let me explain—"

"Bobby." The name felt like an accusation on her tongue. "Why didn't you tell me?"

"It was stupid of me. I just..."

"Lied." Claire's voice was flat. Dead. "The whole time, you knew who I was, and you said nothing."

"I promised to tell you after we caught Derek, remember?" His chest was heaving. As two paramedics rushed in, he waved the one off who tried to look at his wound. "I made you that promise, and I intend to fully keep it. But right now, you need medical attention."

"Screw that." Her voice held just as much anger as it had a few minutes ago. "Last night, you had every opportunity to tell me who you are."

He finally looked at her. "I'm Garrett Cross, not Bobby Anderson. I left Bobby buried with Lily that day at the cemetery. I'll never go back to being that weak kid who caused his sister's death." He hesitated. Blew out a breath. "Or yours."

Something in her already broken heart fissured. "There was nothing you could have done to save Lily."

"Except call her like I always had before." His voice trembled. He blinked rapidly. "I'm sorry," he said. "CJ, I'm so sorry—"

"Don't call me that." Claire's voice was sharp. "Don't you dare call me that. Only Lily called me that."

"I know. I—"

"Sir." The paramedic grabbed Garrett's arm. "Sit down. You're losing a lot of blood. We need to stop it before you pass out."

Officers and federal agents swarmed the cabin. Derek was being dragged away. Vivi was free and hugging her husband. Vivi, who was safe. Alive. Because Claire had fought back and attacked Derek when it mattered most. It had bought enough time for the team to breach.

Not like Lily. This time, Claire had been strong enough.

The realization should have felt like victory. Instead, with Garrett's deception exposed and her heart in pieces, it tasted like ashes.

Claire coughed, gently rubbing her bruised throat. A paramedic began checking her vitals. Claire tried to push the woman away. Vivi touched Claire's shoulder. "You saved my life and helped catch a serial killer. Let the paramedics do their job."

Garrett reached for her. "Please, Claire."

She jerked her arm away from him. Stepped back. "Get away from me." She was shaking now. "Just get away."

"Claire—"

"Get away!"

Ian stepped between them. "Commander. Let's give her space."

She could see he wanted to argue. Wanted to explain. Wanted to make her understand.

She pivoted, found Vivi leaning into Ian's embrace. "I've got you," he said softly to her. "You're safe. I've got you."

Tears sprang into Claire's eyes, seeing their display of love and support. Husband and wife reunited.

The paramedic guided her outside, sat her in the back of an ambulance, and began treating her wound. It all felt far away, surreal.

Not just confronting a serial killer, but all of it. Realizing she'd been the target and Lily had paid the price. That Bobby—Garrett—had deceived her. That Wolf wasn't the man she'd thought he was.

Mill's voice came through the comm. "Station is clear. Repeat, station is clear. Bomb squad is on site. We found the device—crude but effective. If we'd been thirty seconds slower..."

Garrett strode out of the cabin, jaw tight. The paramedic chased after him, insisting he was losing a lot of blood. "But you weren't," he replied to Mills.

"Copy that, Commander. Everyone okay there?"

He met her eyes. Agent Hendricks stepped forward, cutting off her line of sight and asking questions, but Claire couldn't hear them. Couldn't hear anything but Derek's horrible voice.

"Does she know, Bobby? Does Claire know you're Lily's pathetic big brother? That you've been lying to her this whole time?"

"Claire." Garrett was suddenly there, cutting off Hendricks. "Please. Let me explain."

"There's nothing to explain." Her voice was empty. The paramedic gave Garrett a look, then ignored him as she cleaned Claire's wound. It was obvious the poor woman was still listening. "You tricked me. Deceived me. That's all there is to it."

"I was trying to protect you—"

"By lying?" Now she looked at him. "By sleeping with me while pretending to be someone else?"

"I wasn't pretending about my feelings for you."

Claire's laugh was bitter. "Did you enjoy it? Watching me fall apart over your sister? Listening to me talk about that night? Kissing me while you knew exactly who I was?"

"It wasn't like that."

"Then what was it like?" Claire stood, forcing the paramedic to step back. Hendricks turned on her heel and left. Claire was unsteady, but standing. "Tell me, *Bobby*. What was it like?"

"Don't call me that."

"Why not? It's your name, isn't it?" She took a step toward him. Then another. "Bobby Anderson. Age eighteen when Lily died because you had to go out with friends that Sunday night and didn't call her. I barely remember you. But you—" Her voice broke. "You remembered me, didn't you? You knew exactly who I was. And you said nothing."

"You had so much on your mind. I wanted to wait until the proper time."

"When?" She stopped, turned away. "It doesn't matter."

"It matters to me."

"Well, it shouldn't!" She spun back. The anger at Derek morphed into anger at Garrett. It bubbled and ran over, flooding the ground at her feet like quicksand. Everything was wrong. How could she have trusted him? "You lied, Garrett. Or Bobby. Or Wolf. Or whoever the hell you are. You lied about the thing that mattered most."

"I know."

"Then why?" Her voice cracked completely. "Why not tell me the truth from the start?"

Garrett met her eyes. "Because I knew you'd react exactly like this. Because I knew that if you knew I was Bobby, you'd see me as a failure. It's my fault Lily's dead, Claire." He made a fist and slammed it into his chest. "Mine." He took a breath. "And I wanted—just once—to be the person who saved someone instead."

Claire stared at him. Then she shook her head. "You don't get it," she said softly. "You saved me from Derek. But you—" Her voice broke again. "You broke my heart."

He flinched as if the words hit like bullets. "I'm so sorry."

"I don't want to hear it." She caught sight of Ian leading Vivi to a second ambulance. Hendricks stood a respectable distance away, watching Claire carefully as she spoke into her phone. Claire raised her voice. "After I give my statement, I'm heading back to D.C. You can direct further inquiries to me there."

She pushed past Garrett without looking at him. Without saying anything else. At the door of the nearest SUV, she paused.

Derek had been loaded into a sheriff's vehicle, still smiling despite his broken wrist and other injuries. Hendricks caught up to her. "Two deputies will transport him to the county lockup, then to our field office in Missoula tomorrow."

Derek wasn't staring at her, though. "You think she'll forgive you?" Derek called through the glass to Garrett. "She won't. I made sure of that. Even if I go to prison."

He laughed. "I still won because she'll never trust you again. And that—" More laughter. "That's better than killing her. Knowing I screwed you both up for the rest of your lives." Finally, his gaze swung to Claire. "You'll never trust anyone again, and as long as I'm alive, you'll never sleep good. You won't be able to eat. All you'll do is think about me."

She wanted to yank open the door and kill him right there. Instead, she held her ground and watched the vehicle drive away.

Mission accomplished. Derek Sullivan was in custody. Vivi was safe.

And Claire...she was still alive.

CHAPTER FOURTEEN

Garrett had everything he'd wanted except the one thing that mattered most.

As Grizzly drove off with Claire to the station, Ian approached, one arm still around Vivi. "Commander," Vivi started.

"Don't," Garrett said.

"You need to go after her."

"She doesn't want to see me."

"She's in shock," Vivi said. "Traumatized. Give her time—"

"How much?" Garrett finally looked at the two of them. "How much time does it take to forgive someone for deceiving you about something like this?"

They were both quiet. Ian glanced down at Vivi, squeezing her shoulder. She gave him a knowing look. One that said they'd been through rough times like this and still survived. "I don't know," Ian said, "but I know not trying means losing her for sure."

Garrett looked at the road where Claire had disappeared. Special Agent Hendricks was headed back to town, following Claire.

He wasn't one to talk about personal matters, especially not his emotions. Maybe he could blame it on the blood loss. The adrenaline. The world seemed dimmer. There was a ringing in his ears. "Last night, she asked me to tell her everything. She said eventually she needed to know all of me, not just the parts I thought were safe to share."

Vivi quirked a brow. "And you said?"

"I said I would tell her after Derek was caught." Garrett's laugh was bitter. "I said I'd tell her everything."

She gestured at the road. "Then go tell her."

"I tried. She won't listen."

"Then make her listen." Vivi grabbed his forearm. "You made a mistake. A huge one, but Claire needs to know why."

"She knows why. I told her. To protect her from—"

"No." Vivi shook her head. "You told her you wanted to be the person who saved her. But that's not the whole truth, is it?"

Garrett said nothing.

"You loved Lily," Vivi said gently. "And when she died, you blamed yourself. You found out about Claire, the girl who survived. The girl who also tried to protect Lily." She paused. "You didn't just want to save her, Garrett. You needed to. Because saving her meant Lily's death wasn't completely meaningless."

The world shrank. The ringing amped up. He

clutched his wounded side and nearly doubled over. "I failed Lily. I failed CJ."

Vivi's voice was soft. "You didn't fail Claire, Garrett. You saved her."

"That doesn't make it right."

Vivi patted his shoulder. "Give her time. Let her process everything. And then—when she's ready—try again. Tell her the whole truth about why Bobby became Garrett. Why you needed this mission. Why you fell in love with her."

Garrett's throat was tight. "What if she never wants to hear it?"

"Knowing Claire? She will. Eventually. Because despite everything, she loves you, too. I saw it these last few days. The way she looked at you, wanted you by her side."

"And now?"

"Now she's hurt. She rightfully feels betrayed. Angry." Vivi's smile was sad. "But love doesn't die that easily. Trust me."

Garrett wanted to believe her. But when he closed his eyes, all he saw was Claire's face. The moment Derek had said his name. The moment she'd understood exactly who he was.

The moment everything between them had shattered.

The world kept shifting under his feet. Blood loss, the paramedics said, pushing him toward the ambulance. He tried to argue—he'd had worse, could handle it—but Ian's look said he wasn't winning this one. At the hospital, they stitched him up—fifteen sutures but no internal damage. The ER doc gave him a prescription he wouldn't fill and told him to follow up with his family doctor. Through it all, he saw Claire's face—the betrayal in her eyes.

An hour later, he arrived at the police station. The place was chaos—bomb squad vehicles, FBI agents, Local deputies. The press was gathering at the perimeter. Claire was inside, giving her statement. Garrett could see her through the window. Pale but composed. She'd tied a scarf around her neck to hide the bruises Derek's fingers had left.

He stayed outside and let the team handle the debriefing. Let Ian and Vivi deal with the authorities.

Hawk found him by the tactical vehicle. "Commander."

"Hawk."

"Hell of a shot you didn't let me take."

"You said the risk was too high."

"It was." Hawk leaned against the vehicle. "So you went in."

"Had to."

"Yeah." Hawk was quiet for a moment. "For what it's worth? You did the right thing—going in and taking that bastard down. I know you wanted me to take that shot and kill him, but you also wanted Agent Dawson to get her day in court." He jutted his chin toward where Claire was. "Now, she will, thanks to you."

The two of them had only worked together for a few days, and already the man seemed to know him. "It doesn't feel like enough."

"Never does." Hawk stared at the station. "She'll come around. Realize what you did for her."

"You sound like Vivi."

"Doc's smart. You should listen to her."

Garrett said nothing.

They stood there as the sun set over Blackridge. He'd saved Claire and lost her anyway.

Inside the station, she finished her statement, then walked out with Special Agent Hendricks. She saw Garrett standing by the vehicle. For a moment, their eyes met. Then Claire looked away. She got in the FBI vehicle and drove away.

Garrett watched until the taillights disappeared.

"Commander," Lynx called from the station door. "They need your statement."

Blowing out a breath, Garrett walked inside. He gave his report.

Name: Garrett Cross. Commander, Shadow Point Security.

Formerly known as Bobby Anderson. Half-brother of Lily Harper.

The man who'd saved Claire Dawson.

And the man who'd broken her heart.

CHAPTER 15

Three months later
  Virginia

THE VIRGINIA CEMETERY was quiet and peaceful. More park-like than graveyard. Lily would have loved the view.

Garrett stood in front of her headstone, holding yellow tulips—her favorite. Damned impossible to come by in winter, but he had a standing order with a florist. He came here every year on her birthday. Sometimes on the anniversary of her death, too, though that was harder. Heavier.

Today, she would have been twenty-nine. A woman instead of the fourteen-year-old girl frozen in his memory. He tried to imagine her grown up—working, maybe married, definitely still making terrible puns and laughing at her own jokes.

He couldn't. The image wouldn't form.

Lily was forever fourteen. Forever lost. Forever his failure.

"Hey, Lily-bean," he said quietly. The old nickname felt strange on his lips after so many years. "Happy birthday."

The headstone didn't answer. It never did. But Garrett talked anyway, like he always did on these visits.

"I kept my promise." He brushed the powdery snow away, crouched, and placed the tulips at the base of the stone. "I found CJ and protected her from Derek Sullivan—turns out he was there that night. Collin's cousin. He's in federal custody now. The arraignment happened last month. He'll go to trial in a few months and then to prison for the rest of his life. You'd be proud of CJ. She did an amazing job bringing a solid case against him."

The wind rustled through the trees. Birds sang from the skeletal trees.

"She's safe. That's what matters, right?" Garrett's voice cracked. "I saved her. Just like I should have saved you."

But the cost.

Three months. It had been three months since Claire had walked away from him at that police station in Montana. Three months of silence. Of her refusing his calls. Of carefully worded emails from her attorney— because yes, she'd gotten an attorney to handle any communication related to Derek's case.

Please direct all inquiries through counsel.

Professional. Distant. Final.

"I screwed up, Lil," Garrett said. He stayed crouched, staring at the headstone. "I lied to her about who I was. About you. About everything that mattered." He laughed bitterly. "You'd be so disappointed in me."

Lily had always been the honest one. The one who told the truth even when it hurt. Even when it would have been easier to lie.

Garrett had hidden. Had told himself it was for Claire's protection, for the mission, for all sorts of noble-sounding reasons that were really just cowardice.

"I fell in love with her," he said quietly. "Your best friend. CJ. She's... She's incredible. Smart and strong and brave. She saved Dr. Montgomery, the psychologist on my team. Fought off Derek with her hands zip-tied. She's not the scared kid from that night. She's—" His voice broke. "She's everything. And I lost her because I was too afraid to tell her the truth when I should have. I'm not Bobby anymore, and I just couldn't admit it until it was too late."

Christmas was everywhere, even here in the cemetery, with pine wreaths and red and green bows. But not in his heart. That was forever frozen in Montana—in the moment Claire had looked at him like he was a stranger.

"I don't know how to fix it," he said. "Doc says to give her time. That she'll come around." He looked at Lily's name carved in granite. Traced it with his fingertip. "But what if she doesn't? What if I broke something that can't be repaired?"

The cemetery was still quiet. Still peaceful. Still offering no answers.

Garrett stood. Brushed snow from his gloves. "I should go. I just wanted to... I wanted you to know I kept my promise. CJ's alive. Safe. That has to be enough."

Even if it felt like nothing at all.

"Bobby?"

Garrett froze.

That voice. He'd know it anywhere. In his dreams. In his nightmares. In every quiet moment of the past three months.

He turned.

Claire stood twenty feet away, holding yellow tulips. For a long moment, they just stared at each other.

She looked different. Thinner, maybe. Tired. Her hair was shorter—cut to her shoulders instead of past them. She was wearing jeans and a wool peacoat, not the professional suits he'd seen her in.

But her eyes were the same. Blue. Guarded. Looking at him like she wasn't sure if she should stay or run.

"CJ," Garrett said. Then caught himself. "Claire. I'm sorry. I didn't—"

"I come here every year," she interrupted. "On the anniversary of her death. But this year, I decided it was time to celebrate her life instead. I didn't know you'd be here." She looked at the flowers in her hand. "I should have realized you would."

"I can go," Garrett said. "Give you space. I don't want to—"

"Don't." Claire took a step forward. "Don't go. We should... We should talk."

Garrett's heart hammered against his ribs, hope soaring even as he tried to shut it down. "Okay."

Claire walked to Lily's grave and placed her tulips next to his. They both stood there, looking at the headstone. At the name. At the dates that were too close together.

"I testified at Derek's preliminary hearing," Claire said finally. "You probably know that."

"I did."

"He pleaded not guilty. The trial's set for June."

"That's good."

"I'll have to testify again in detail. About that night. About everything." Claire's voice was quiet. "I'm not looking forward to it."

"You'll be strong," Garrett said. "Like you always are."

Claire peeked at him from the corner of her eye. "I wasn't strong that night in Montana. I was terrified. I thought he was going to kill Vivi. That I was going to watch someone else I cared about die."

"But you fought anyway. That's what strength is."

"I fought because I remembered what it felt like to be helpless. To watch Lily die and not be able to stop it." Claire's voice cracked. "I couldn't let that happen again. Not to Vivi. Not to anyone. I got angry, like you told me to. It worked."

"You saved her," Garrett said. "You attacked Derek

when it mattered and bought time for us to breach. That was all you."

"He was choking me. I was losing consciousness. You pulled him off. You..." She heaved a deep sigh. "You saved me."

"We saved each other."

Claire was quiet for a moment. "Why didn't you tell me?"

The question he'd been dreading for three months.

"Because I was a coward," Garrett said. "Because I knew if I told you I was Bobby, you'd see me as the failure I was." He paused. "And I wanted—just once—to be the hero instead. To keep you safe. To make up for not being there for you and my sister when I should have been."

"It's not the whole truth, though. Is it?" Claire turned to face him fully. "Vivi came to see me a few weeks ago when she was in town. She told me something."

Garrett's chest tightened. "What?"

"She said that saving me wasn't just about you being a hero. It was about Lily. About making her death mean something." Claire's eyes were wet. "She said you needed to protect me because if you did, then Lily's sacrifice wasn't for nothing."

Garrett couldn't speak. Couldn't breathe.

"Is that true?" Claire asked. "Did you take the mission because of Lily?"

He could lie. Could deny it. Could make it about duty or honor or professional obligation. But he'd lied to her enough.

"Yes," Garrett said. "When Vivi showed me your file and told me what was happening, I knew I had to be the one to protect you. Because you tried to save my sister. And if I could keep you alive, then maybe—" His voice broke.

Claire was crying now. Silent tears tracking down her face. "So it *was* about Lily. Not about me."

Garrett stepped closer. "It was about both of you. The moment I met you in Montana, I realized you weren't just Lily's best friend anymore. You were brilliant and brave and strong. You were the woman who'd survived hell and built a career catching monsters. You were—" He stopped. "You were everything. And I fell in love with you."

"You lied," Claire said. Her voice was thick. "You slept with me while lying about who you were."

"I was selfish," Garrett said. "I wanted you so badly that I convinced myself the lie didn't matter. That I could tell you after." He looked at his boots, at the frozen ground. "There's no excuse, Claire. I deceived you, I hurt you, and I'm sorry. More sorry than I can ever express."

She was quiet for a long time. Long enough that Garrett thought she might just walk away. Leave him standing at Lily's grave with his apology and his regrets. "Do you know the other reason I decided to come here on her birthday instead of the anniversary of her death?"

Garrett looked up, shook his head.

"Because I don't want to remember the worst day of her life. I want to remember her living, laughing. Being Lily." Claire pointed at the headstone. "She was so full of life, even at fourteen. She loved boy bands and that silly bird game app. She wanted to save all the animals." A sob broke through. "And Derek and Collin took all of that away. Because they wanted to hurt me."

"It's not your fault."

"I know. Logically, I know. I've been in therapy again since Montana. Three times a week." Claire laughed softly. "Dr. Nunnely says I have PTSD. Survivor's guilt. Trust issues." She looked at Garrett. "Abandonment issues, too. Because apparently, everyone I care about either dies or lies to me."

The words cut deep.

"Claire—"

She held up a hand. "I'm not trying to hurt you. I'm just—" She shook her head. "I'm being honest about how I feel about what you did." She paused. "I loved you, whoever you are now. *I loved you.* And when Derek said your name, when I realized you'd been deceiving me the whole time..." She pressed a hand to her chest. "It felt like dying. Like losing Lily all over again. Like I couldn't trust my own judgment anymore."

"I'm so sorry."

"I know you are." Claire wiped her face. "But sorry doesn't fix it. Sorry doesn't make me trust you again."

Garrett's throat was tight. "That's totally fair."

"But," Claire said, and his heart stuttered, "Vivi said something else when she came to see me. She said that what we had is worth fighting for." She looked at him. "Is it? Is it worth fighting for?"

"Yes," Garrett said without hesitation. "If you'll let me, I'll spend the rest of my life proving it to you."

"How?"

"However you need me to. Therapy. Time. Space."

"I feel like I don't know you."

"You don't. But I want you to. I joined the Navy and became a SEAL. I spent fifteen years learning how to protect people. How to be strong enough that no one I cared about would die on my watch again." Garrett's voice was rough. "And then Vivi showed up with your file."

"So you took the mission."

"I demanded the mission. Told Vivi if anyone else ran point, I'd quit." He looked at Claire. "Then I met you, and you were so much more than I expected. Stronger. Smarter. More beautiful." He paused. "I was terrified that if you knew who I was, you'd see me as Bobby, so I didn't tell you. I told myself it was to protect the mission, to keep you focused, but really—" His voice cracked. "Really, I was just scared you'd reject me if you knew the truth."

"I might have," Claire said quietly. "At first. The guilt about Lily—about surviving when she didn't—it's shaped my whole life. If I'd known you were her brother..." She trailed off. "I don't know how I would have reacted."

"That's what I told myself. That I was protecting you from that conflict." Garrett met her eyes. "But I was wrong. You deserved the truth. Deserved to make your own choice. I took that from you, and know it was wrong."

Claire looked at Lily's grave. At the tulips they'd both brought. "She would have liked you. The you that you are now. Garrett."

"You think so?"

"She always said her brother was too serious. Too hard on himself." Claire smiled slightly. "She'd probably tease you about the codename. 'Wolf? Really, Bobby? That's so dramatic.'"

Garrett laughed despite himself. "Yeah. She would."

"I requested a transfer," Claire said. "To the Missoula FBI field office."

Garrett's heart stopped. "What?"

"It was approved last week. I start the first of January." She looked at him. "I'm moving to Montana."

The sun felt warmer on his face. "Why?"

"Because Shadow Point Security is there, and a certain commander whom I'm still angry with and who I don't completely trust yet is, too. But who I—" She stopped. "Who I'm not ready to give up on."

Hope flared in Garrett's chest. "That's...more than I deserve."

"It is, and I need time," she said quickly. "And honesty. Complete honesty. No more secrets. No more lies—even the ones you think are protecting me."

"No more secrets," Garrett agreed. "I promise."

"I mean it. If we do this—if we try—you have to be all in. No holding back. No 'I'll tell her later.' Everything."

"Everything," he said, nodding like he'd lost his senses. "I'm Garrett Cross. Former Navy SEAL. Commander of Shadow Point Security. Brother of Lily

Harper. And I'm in love with Claire Dawson. Have been since the moment she learned her call sign was Paperclip and looked like she wanted to fight me about it."

Claire laughed. The sound was like sunshine after rain. "I hate that call sign."

"I know. That's why I like it."

"Fury," she corrected. "Remember? You said you'd change it."

"Let's hope you never need a call sign with my team again."

They stood there in the cemetery, tulips at Lily's grave, the sun warming the air around them.

"I'm scared," Claire said quietly. "Scared of being hurt again."

"I know," Garrett said. "I'm scared too. Scared I'll screw this up. Scared I'll lose you again." He held out his hand. "But I think Doc is right. What we have is worth fighting for."

Claire looked at his hand. At his face. At Lily's grave.

She slid her hand into his. "Okay," she said. "Let's try. But Garrett—"

"Yeah?"

"If you ever lie to me again, I will make you regret it. Professionally and personally."

"Understood."

"I'm not joking."

"I know you're not, and I believe you."

Claire smiled. Small but real. "Good."

They stood there, hands linked, at Lily's grave. Not quite healed. But maybe on their way.

"Thank you," Garrett said to the headstone. To Lily. To whoever might be listening. "For giving me this second chance. For—" His voice broke. "For everything."

The wind rustled through the trees.

And Garrett could have sworn he heard Lily laughing.

EPILOGUE

Six Months Later
Montana

"FURY, I need your help on a case."

Claire looked up from her desk at the Missoula FBI field office to see Garrett standing in her doorway. He was wearing tactical pants and a Shadow Point polo, looking every inch the commander.

Looking like home.

"Don't call me that," she said, fighting a smile.

"It suits you."

"I'm Special Agent Dawson."

Garrett stepped into her office and closed the door. "Special Agent Dawson, Shadow Point Security requests your consultation on a serial arson case. Three fires in the past month. All targeting women's shelters."

Claire's professional interest sparked. "Missoula?"

"Helena. But the arsonist is escalating. We think he'll move locations soon."

"Send me the files. I'll review tonight."

"Tonight you have dinner with me."

"Do I?"

"You do. I made reservations at that Italian place you like."

Claire raised an eyebrow. "Presumptuous."

"Hopeful." Garrett's smile was warm. Real. The smile he only gave her. "What do you say, CJ?"

She should probably still object to the nickname. Should maintain some professional boundaries.

But they'd been together for six months now. Really together. Honest together. She'd moved into his place last month—a cabin outside Missoula with a view of the mountains and enough space for them both.

Therapy was helping. Dr. Nunnely via video call three times a week. Couples counseling once a week with Dr. Montgomery—Vivi, who'd become more than a psychologist. She was a friend.

Derek's trial had happened two weeks ago. Claire had testified. Garrett had sat in the courtroom every single day, supporting her silently from the gallery. Derek had been convicted on all counts. Life in prison, no parole.

It was over.

And Claire was finally, finally healing. "Okay," she said. "Dinner. But I'm still reviewing those files tonight."

"I'm counting on it." Garrett moved closer. Leaned against her desk. "I love you, you know."

"I know."

"Do you? Because I don't say it enough."

"You say it every day."

"Still not enough." He reached out and tucked a strand of hair behind her ear. "I love you, Claire Dawson. Former Paperclip. Current Fury. Future—" He stopped. Smiled. "Future consultant for Shadow Point Security?"

Vivi had been relentlessly recruiting her. "Maybe. If the pay is right."

"We'll negotiate."

Claire stood. Walked around her desk. "I don't work cheap, Commander."

"Wouldn't dream of it." Garrett pulled her close. Kissed her forehead. "See you tonight?"

"See you tonight."

He started to leave, then paused at the door. "Hey, Claire?"

"Yeah?"

"Thank you for giving me a second chance. For trusting me again." His voice was soft. "I know it wasn't easy."

"No," Claire agreed, "it wasn't. But you were worth fighting for."

Garrett's smile could have lit the entire office. "So were you."

He left. Claire sat back down at her desk. Before she started working, she looked at the photo on her desk. Two photos, actually. Side by side in a double frame.

On the left was Lily, laughing at something off-camera. On the right were Claire and Garrett, taken last month at Ian and Vivi's anniversary party. Claire's head on Garrett's shoulder. His arm around her waist. Both of them smiling.

Happy.

Healing.

Home.

"I love your brother, Lily," Claire whispered. "I think I'm going to propose to him."

And somehow—impossibly—she could have sworn she felt her best friend smile.

Ready to find out what happens next?
Click here to get your copy of Shadow Target so you can keep the romance and adventure going with Hawk and his second chance romance, close proximity HEA!
And be sure to sign up for my reader newsletter so you're the first to know about new releases, giveaways, and other cool stuff!
Sign me up! Misty's Newsletter!

VISIT MY STORE

Did you know you can buy directly from me? When you do, the retailer doesn't take a cut and I can pass on the savings to YOU!

https://mistyevansbooks.com/shop

Benefits:

You can find ALL my books in one place

SAVE money

EARLY access to new releases

Special Collections, Boxed eSets, and Limited Editions

Support a small business (and support a dream!)

Why Buy Direct?

When you purchase a book by your favorite author, electronic or print, on retailer platforms, the company keeps 30-70% of the sale, leaving the author with little to no profit (after the company deducts delivery fees, taxes, and other fees).

Buying directly from the author means that more goes to them so they can keep turning out stories for you. Every published story, every book, requires cover art, editing, and hours and hours of the author's time simply to create it. Not to mention overhead costs, such as websites, newsletters, writing software, graphics programs, advertising, taxes, etc.

In addition, one of the big-name retailers requires exclusivity, and all of them have terms of service and rules and regulations that make it challenging and time-consuming for an indie author to navigate the publishing world.

Most of us would MUCH rather spend our time creating more stories for YOU, rather than trying to jump through the hoops at the retailers. Buying direct from your favorite authors (where available) helps ensure that an author you love is not subject to unexplained account closures, withholding of royalties, censorship, and other issues that can affect their livelihood.

I've experienced ALL of these. By buying direct, you help put control of my work back in my hands - and I can continue to write more.

Either way, thank you for supporting me! I understand buying direct doesn't work for everyone and even if you use the retailers to buy my books, I appreciate you!

Happy reading,

Misty

https://mistyevansbooks.com/shop

MEET MISTY

USA TODAY Bestselling Author Misty Evans is celebrating her 100th published novel in 2025. She loves writing romantasy, urban fantasy, paranormal romance, and mystery/suspense. Under her pen name, Nyx Halliwell, she also writes supernatural cozy mysteries.

When not reading or writing (which is most of the time), she enjoys music, movies, and hanging out with her husband, twin sons, and three spoiled rescue dogs. She's a crafter at heart and has far too many projects to finish.

Visit www.mistyevansbooks.com to check out her online store and sign up for her newsletter.

NOTE FROM MISTY

Thank you for reading this story! It is an honor and a privilege to write books for you. I'm an indie author, and every fan is important to me. I pour my heart into each story and do my best to bring you an escape from the real world.

Readers are the key to my success - not a traditional publishing deal (I've had four), an agent (I've had two), or a publicity team (yes, you guessed it, I've had several of those as well.)

Those of you who read my books, love my characters and worlds, and then tell others about them are the best of friends. I adore you and will keep writing if you keep reading!

If you'd like to learn about my other books, sales, and special promotions, please sign up for my newsletter at **www.mistyevansbooks.com**. You'll receive FREE series starters from me.

Support me directly (no retailer taking their cut), grab special edition box sets, and get new releases before they are out at retailers by visiting my store **https://mistyevansbooks.com/shop**.

I have sales and offer NEW RELEASES early! Check it out.

Last but not least, if you enjoy clean, cozy mysteries, visit my pen name **www.nyxhalliwell.com** to see those books.

Thank you, and happy reading!
Misty